A HANDFUL OF HEXES

THE WITCH OF HENBANE ISLAND
BOOK 4

PERRY WILSON

Jeremy R. Strong

THE TETHERING
BOOK 1 – BOUND BY BLOOD

DOUBLE DRAGON

Ebook ISBN: 978-1-990509-48-3
Paperback ISBN: 978-1-990509-47-6
Audio book ISBN:978-1-990509–49-0

Cover created by Getcovers

FREE BOOK

Claim your copy of Magic Will Out when you sign up for my newsletter and follow Cossi as she seeks answers to her past. Use the QR code to claim your copy now.

1

The last month was a whirlwind of getting the Inner Spell ready to open. Elias was true to his word and finished his part a week ago. Since then, I'd put together more beds, wardrobes, and shelving than I'd done in my entire life so far. Lance had made me the tables and chairs, and everyone helped. Even with so many hands, I was exhausted every night.

Now, I was ready. The website was up on the paranormal social media platforms, and here I was, sitting at my laptop and waiting for the first call. The Equinox festival was a week away and everyone was busy preparing. I couldn't decide if it would be tacky to distribute flyers during the event or not. Of course, it would help if I had my head around what exactly went on.

My familiar was no help. Destroyer told me he'd be resting then because too many witches were noisy and got in his way. My friends said there would be games and feasts. And a market, which is why the residents were preparing so early. Some demonstrations were scheduled, but the festival was mostly an excuse to socialize.

I couldn't bring myself to ask about dancing around the bonfire in the nude because maybe that was a stereotype or just a Wiccan thing, but mostly to keep the image Mrs. V naked out of my brain.

That was a problem for a week from now. Today, I could enjoy the peace up here at The Inner Spell. The villages were all bustling with deliveries and talks about the arrangements or the booth locations. Here, other than the occasional bike taking mysterious boxes to the Earth witches, no one came by unannounced.

My phone rang.

Phillip. He usually didn't reach out now that Mrs. V was my mentor and he was only my landlord.

"The Inner Spell, how may I make your life easier?" Corny, but I was trying out some greetings.

"Cossi, the festival committee needs your booth details by end of day."

He said he wasn't upset that he got fired as my mentor, but he didn't bother with any small talk since the announcement. I tried not to take it personally.

"I get a booth?" A thrill went through me. The witches recognized my business as worthy of being part of the festival.

"Yes. I'm surprised you didn't already know that. What size will you need?"

So, by tonight, he meant right now.

"I guess, big enough for me and a few brochures. Maybe a basket of samples. Like the soap from Mr. Macy. Some teas from the Earth witches."

He gave a grunt. "Small. You need to send them a one-page plan." He ended the call, like he was too busy to say goodbye.

I'd been thinking of moving up to The Inner Spell since it was habitable, but Mrs. V said I shouldn't isolate myself. Like a short ride from the village would get in anyone's way. Maybe Phillip was busy. At home he still made me the occasional sandwich, and he was always ready with a cup of tea. We didn't talk much, but before that, he'd only really engaged me when he was teaching me how to run a business.

Mrs. Vestum was a very different experience. She gave me hours of magic training every day. I had the time, and I really enjoyed learning spells. I was pretty good at casting even some of the more complex ones. What no one seemed to be ready to teach me was how to fit in.

My friends tried, but since they grew up here and I grew up on the mainland in a nonmagical world, the gap was so big we didn't know how to cross it. I didn't know when to ask questions, and they didn't know what I assumed.

I closed my eyes and practiced a calming mantra. Not magic, but still it worked.

I would find my place on Henbane.

I would find my third power.

I would succeed at my business.

My phone rang again.

Not from someone in my contacts. Normally I would ignore the call. D had loaded every Henbane contact in my phone. Not every paranormal contact in the world, so since my number was the business one, now I'd be answering a lot of spam calls. Even D didn't have a reliable way to block those.

"The Inner Spell. How can I make your life serene?" No, I didn't like that one at all.

"The new place on Henbane, right? I have the right

number?" It was a woman's voice, breathless in a way that indicated flustered rather than sultry.

"You have the right number. What can I do for you today?"

"Look, I know you don't list it as a B&B, but I've always wanted to come to Henbane for the festival. But I don't have relatives or friends there. So, I can't get a place to stay."

She paused. I guess I was supposed to make the connection. It wasn't a big leap. "You want to stay here for the festival?"

"If that's okay. I'm happy to pay."

My first booking. Henbane didn't have any hotels or guest houses. They didn't want a tourist economy, but this caller was right. If anyone wanted to come to the festival, they needed to know someone here.

"Yes, let me get your details."

Her name was Zinnia Flor and she booked one of the chalets. I charged half the price I listed for the space's real use.

"There isn't much in the way of food service," I said.

"That's fine, dear. I can ride into the village for meals. I'll see you in a few days. I'm so looking forward to exploring before the festival starts. I'm so excited. I've wanted to do this for years."

One guest who would happily take care of herself. I couldn't stop grinning. I would have something to tell D, Lilibeth, and Lance when we had lunch.

I checked the social media account for the inn. A few more posts showing the surroundings and announcing the opening would help get more customers.

I already had a heart on the last post I'd put up. And a comment. Ms. Zinnia Flor had told everyone I was taking reservations for the festival.

Having one guest was different from having a full house. The council had not approved the site for a B&B. I would need to make sure I wasn't going to run into problems on day one of my new life.

By the time I headed back to my room at the bookstore, I had reservations for all six of the chalets and a list of things to get so the guests enjoyed their stay. Thank goodness Elias had suggested we add another to make an even number. Otherwise, I'd have to turn down one reservation. The main building still needed a bit of prep before I put guests in there.

The top of the list of things I had to get on right away was making up some welcome gifts, which would hold a variety of the island's products. I could take the idea into my real business. No reason a witch who came to meditate or experiment didn't need to feel welcome.

I parked Beulah in the bike lot and headed toward Phillip's place. Ahead, Mark came out of Mr. Macy's tea and potions store talking to someone on his phone.

He didn't notice me, so I kept going. We'd been on a couple more dates in the weeks since we'd caught the killer. Between Mark and D, my love life was more active than it had been before I knew I was a witch.

Both men were great in different ways. Mark had a

secret, and I was sure we could help him if he just asked. And D was open and always ready to dive in and have fun. Even though the residents of Henbane didn't have the hangups about relationships that nonmagical humans did, I really had to choose one. But I wasn't ready. I didn't know if that was to choose, or to have a relationship go deeper than the occasional date.

Mark stepped around the back of Raziel's books to the little courtyard I used when I wanted to think or talk to my familiar, Destroyer. It was also where the door leading to the apartment opened. If he was looking for privacy, I didn't want to barge in. I swear I wasn't snooping, but I needed to know when the call ended.

I leaned against the wall and looked through my phone as I waited for the sound of conversation to stop.

I really tried, but when you hear your name pop out of the background noise, it's impossible not to focus in on the conversation.

"Cossi doesn't know."

That's what got my attention. What particular thing on the billions of 'Cossi doesn't know' list was he talking about?

"I know, it looks like she thinks the killings are all connected. But not about you. Even I don't know who you are. She thinks it's her mother's doing."

It wasn't? Now I stopped pretending I was trying to give him his privacy.

"I will tell you if it changes. I know. You don't have to remind me. If I don't act normal, someone will notice."

He paused to listen.

"No one wants that. If she finds you, she finds all the secrets. No, I will not put us at risk."

Then he swore.

I stuck my phone up at my face just in case he came back to the street.

"If you don't let me do what I'm good at, it will all fall apart."

The last wasn't part of a conversation. From what I'd heard, whoever was on the call wouldn't put up with such a bold statement.

I peeked to see if it was safe to head in and saw Mark staring at his phone.

"Hi," I said. Did I sound like I'd just seen him, a little surprised? Or would he guess I'd been listening? Oh, I forgot his power. He'd know if I lied. Note to self, ask Mrs. Vestum for the shielding spells.

"Cossi. I wanted to ask you about the festival."

I didn't need his power to tell me he was lying. Even without my ability to read emotions, his efforts to hide his anger were plain in the tightness of his mouth.

"Sure. I've booked all of the chalets for visitors. I'm really looking forward to it."

"Will you go with me?"

"D already asked me," I said. *But we probably needed to cancel it because I'd be tied up working my booth.*

"Oh, okay. If you're bringing strangers to the island, I'll be working to make sure nothing goes wrong anyway. Maybe we can do something after the excitement dies down."

"Yes. But I don't know when I'll be free. I'm going to be busy with my guests."

The worst conversation we'd ever had. Both of us were hiding something. My secret was that I couldn't trust him after overhearing him. His? I didn't really have a clue.

"I have to go," he said.

"Wait. Do you know if I need to get permission to have guests? I mean, it's not the original purpose?"

"I think the council will be happy you're making money," he said. "Phillip will probably be the right one to ask. He's a business owner and a council member."

He had a point, and I didn't know why I was trying to make this awkward moment last longer. We couldn't possibly need a murder to be comfortable with each other.

"Good idea," I said. "I should probably ask now, just in case I have to get an exception."

"Okay. See you around." He walked away without another word.

"You want me to follow him?" Destroyer spoke in my mind.

I looked around, but he wasn't about to stick his talons in my skin to land. "No. What are you up to?"

"Doing crow things," he said. "Congratulations on the strangers. Please let them know that they are allowed to feed the crows. And if you have any trouble with permission, we are happy to do some revenge bombing."

I assured him I didn't need that kind of help and climbed the stairs to the apartment. Time to talk to Phillip, even though he'd been kind of ignoring me for a while.

"Cossi, I was hoping to catch you," Phillip said as I stepped through the door.

This was the first time since he'd been removed as my mentor that he seemed glad to see me.

"I've been at The Inner Spell. People have been booking me up for the festival," I said.

"Good to hear. The festival is what I wanted to speak about. Well, it's festival related. I have a friend coming early and he will need a place to stay."

I smiled at him because I wasn't sure if he was suggesting I move out to accommodate this friend, or he was suggesting the friend stay with me. If I guessed wrong, it could turn his mood back to the silent treatment and sulking.

"He'll stay here," Phillip said, "in the second bedroom. I just thought you should be aware someone will be with us."

"Thank you," I said. "What's his name?"

"Of course, I should have said that first. Martin Light. He's an earth witch and an old friend. He moved away ages ago to research some kind of historical event."

Phillip's mood must be about the visit. It would be nice to have someone for him to talk to. I wasn't here much, but it's not great to feel like you aren't wanted. I knew it could just be my interpretation, but the timing of his attitude change toward me was suspiciously right after Mrs. V took on my training.

"That's a small room," I said. "I have space at The Inner Spell. Either I can move up there and he can use my room, or I can book him in."

Phillip turned away and put the kettle on for tea.

"That's kind of you," he said with his back to me. "He wouldn't be comfortable moving you out. And I'm looking forward to his visit. But thank you for the offer."

I guess I could understand. I didn't really want to move all my stuff out for a couple of weeks, and I didn't know if it would affect the spell bag. If I moved it, would that mean the protection would go away? I'd gotten used to knowing that my space was just mine. No one could enter, not even if I invited them. Only me.

"Have you eaten?" Phillip asked. "I can make some sandwiches."

"I'll have some of that tea," I said. "I'm not really hungry. And now I have a ton of work to do before people start arriving."

"You have a week," Phillip said. "The festival doesn't start until then."

"My first guest arrives in two days," I said.

I knew I shouldn't brag, but who else starts a business and is successful day one? "I think they plan to make it a bit of a vacation. Meet some people, make friends for next year."

"I see." He poured water in the teapot. "Did you talk to

the council about this change in plans? We approved your license for a meditation and experimentation retreat."

"I don't intend to make tourists a part of my plans," I said. "Surely this is just a special situation. Are you okay with it?"

He handed me a mug of tea. The aroma from the leaves was licorice and berry. It would go really well with the tang of ginger I caught as he opened the cookie tin.

"As a temporary thing, yes. We are protective of our island, you know that. Tourism brings problems."

"I'll talk to Mrs. V about getting approval," I said.

The biggest part of me was sure they'd be okay with it. The problem was that little voice inside reciting all the repercussions if the council decided no. Not only would I disappoint the people who'd booked with me, but my reputation would take a hit. The Inner Spell would struggle to get going if it started out with bad reviews.

"Do it today, if you can," Phillip said. "Drink your tea first. You look like you need a refresher after your busy day."

"Is your friend going to be visiting while he's here?" I needed to know if I was going to encounter him every time I came home.

"He doesn't know many people here anymore," Phillip said. He offered me a ginger cookie and put a handful on a plate. "He's very shy and didn't have many friends before. He didn't grow up here, you see."

Interesting. Why did I assume he was a resident? Oh, because Phillip said Martin left Henbane.

"I'll try not to intrude on your visit," I said.

"You don't have to live in your room, Cossi. I'm sure Martin will be fine if you join us for a meal or two. You and I have been strangers these last few weeks. You've been busy with opening your business, and without our magic lessons, there's been nothing to make us socialize. I'm sorry for that."

One of the reasons Mrs. V took over my mentorship was because Phillip never gave me magic lessons. Was he remembering differently? Did I miss some subtle magical content? He'd given me books, but only kids' ones. Mrs. V was driving me through a curriculum that had me reading spells and lists of powers for what felt like half my day.

"I miss our talks too," I said. "Okay, I'll try not to get in the way of your reunion, but I'll be here a bit more than I have been."

"And maybe don't lock yourself behind the protection spell when you are here. I fear you're turning into a bit of a hermit."

He smiled as he said it, but there was something in his tightly shielded emotions that felt like burning rubber tire. This was something Mrs. V taught me. Yes, people could shield so I couldn't read their emotions clearly, but strong ones seeped through the spell. I had no idea what the smells really meant, but every time something did come through, I made a mental note to get to the source.

I understood why people shielded, and I didn't want to violate their right to privacy, but I needed to know about my powers.

The third one was still hidden from me despite people telling me whatever had blocked it should be fading.

When my business was up and running smoothly, I would have more time to dig into the secrets that got in my way. When the rush from the festival was over, I'd start with my third power. Then I would get to the bottom of what really happened twenty years ago when my parents took me and fled Henbane.

Right now, I had to contact Mrs. V about the council and get through the reading assignment so I could practice the spells she'd mentioned. I wouldn't let anything get in the way of learning to use magic. It was the biggest barrier to me feeling settled here on Henbane.

4

The council not only approved my request to act as a B&B for the festival, but they also added it to the license. They must have had a solid reason, but I chose not to ask and possibly make them change their minds.

Now, The Inner Spell was the only official inn on the island, and I had another income stream to build up funds. I could start to pay the council back for all the expenses I'd run up since arriving. I didn't know how much it was, but I trusted that someone did and that we could set up a schedule. I'd managed to get my degree without student loans, and I wasn't going to start building debt now.

It took a few days, but I was ready, and the first guest was arriving today. Along with my lessons with Mrs. Vestum and my training with Destroyer, apparently I also needed to set up some kind of economic fee structure with the island's animal population rather than just handing out food when I got information. Not that I'd need that in the future because no one would be murdered. Destroyer was certain that my search for the truth about my mother's mistake would only be successful if I let him marshal the birds to find clues, but I wasn't ready yet. After the festival. That's when we could start finding the owners of the remaining talismans.

"Cossi." Mrs. V's voice cut through my daydreaming. "We have an hour of practice before the boat arrives with your guest. Focus."

We were sitting in her kitchen, at the table facing the woods out back of her property. Most of the island's homes had a similar view. Even my bedroom faced a forest. The front of Main Street was free of shrubs or flowers, but almost every other empty space was cultivated by the earth witches to produce some kind of flora.

"There are ten ways to develop a protection spell." I put my finger on the notes I'd taken. "The one Mark gave me is the highest level, and if I want to deactivate it, I will need to open the bag and scatter the contents on a fire."

"I think you should keep it active," she said. "Having a private space right now is probably best. What if you have notes and clues to store?"

I would probably do it electronically. D could set up the firewall and stuff.

"Not everything will be in a form you can put in a database," she said like she could read my mind. I was pretty sure she didn't have that power, but as the protector, maybe her magic adapted to what was needed.

"Do you have a place I could use?"

"I have a protected storage area. You are not welcome to use it. Find a place at The Inner Spell, a room you keep for yourself in that main building, perhaps. Use Mark's spell bag there. Create others with less power for other uses."

I liked the suggestion. It made me feel like I wasn't wasting magic, like it was a nonrenewable resource. "It is nice to know my room is safe," I said. "Phillip's friend arrived yesterday. Staying in the other bedroom."

"I didn't know Phillip had friends outside Henbane," she said. "Who is it?"

"Some old witch named Martin Light. He's super shy. I only met him because he came at lunchtime. If he's come out of his room since then, I'd be surprised."

"Let's use this as an opportunity," Mrs. V said, closing her notebook. "What can we learn about Martin and Phillip from our online sources?"

It felt intrusive, but she was right. If I had any chance of figuring out the whole conspiracy around the event that sent my family off-island, I would need to know how to use the tools available.

"I could have a bird follow him around," I said. "Practice their skills of observing what we need."

"We are not in need of practice," Destroyer said in my mind.

I told Mrs. V what he said.

"Perhaps they already are following people around," she said. "Would we notice?"

"The protector is right," Destroyer said.

I confirmed her guess.

"We're walking a thin line between using this Martin Light as a teaching tool and invading his privacy," she said. "You will need to find your own boundaries."

"I try not to read people," I said. "Some are good at shielding, some not so much. That reminds me. Elias doesn't seem to have any. Emotions, I mean."

"There are various ways to block someone," Mrs. Vestum said in her lecturing voice. "Those who seem better at it may be carrying a ward, like the spell bag. Others use discipline, and that's what allows for slips of emotion, I imagine. There are people with natural shielding from their powers. You may eventually find a way around that type of block. Like I said, you must find your own boundaries. And some powers are fueled by emotion. Not everyone knows about Elias, so I will not violate his privacy."

Since my powers were developing without effort from me, I wasn't sure that my boundaries were the issue. "And this new thing, where I see colors for emotions? You said it was me getting seated in the magic. What if I have no way of enforcing my barriers?"

"We will get to that if it happens," she said. "For now, let's see what we can find out about Mr. Light and Phillip Raziel."

When I first arrived, Mrs. V used that same tone when she said my name. A bit mean and sour. Apparently, I was off that list, whatever it was, and Phillip was on it.

It didn't take that long to find out that the two witches met at a conference three years ago. Martin worked with a small family of foragers. His job was enhancing the properties of the herbs and other plant parts so they would survive shipping. I found his name on a series of research papers covering all kinds of topics.

"No other presence," I said. "I guess his shyness keeps him off the usual 'share everything about your life' media." Most witches did have what I would call a social media presence beyond their business or area of expertise, but nothing like normal humans.

"That conference is held yearly," she said. "It seems like the only interactions they had. I wonder how they became more than just acquaintances."

I'd do a little snooping at home. Nothing magical. My phone rang with an alarm. "I have to go greet Ms. Flor and take her out to the chalet."

"I think your business will change the island," she said as I grabbed my jacket. "It may be for the better. Having new witches to talk to and new ideas. Living in a community surrounded by mundane humans is very different. I fear we have become too distant from the challenges of such a life."

I smiled at her implied compliment.

"Of course, the opposite is true," she said. "The council will be watching to ensure approving The Inner Spell was not a dangerous mistake."

And that was classic Mrs. V.

5

My other guests were arriving in a couple of days, so Ms. Flor had the entire site to herself. She took pictures of her chalet and the welcome gift I'd put together. She was tall and elegantly thin. Her blue-dyed hair hung loose over her shoulders, and her clothes reminded me of old fashioned psychics, all flowing and layered.

"You can use the bike for your full stay," I reminded her. "If you need anything, you have my number. The kitchen isn't open yet, but someone will drop off a breakfast tray in the morning."

"Lovely," she said. "I'll use the map to wander around. I might walk over to the earth witch village this afternoon."

"Lots to explore," I said. "If you don't know anyone on the island, I can make some introductions." A few of the residents had offered their services as guides when they heard I was booking rooms.

"Perhaps tomorrow," she said. "I'm fine on my own, dear. I promise I won't bother some of the famous witches."

We had famous witches?

She must have noticed my shocked face, because I felt embarrassment flow from her.

"I'm so sorry. I forgot your story. You know so little about us. Yes. Henbane is a bit of a legendary place, and a few of its inhabitants are celebrities, I suppose."

"Who? I might be able to make connections for you." Maybe tell her where to find people, or is that not cool? I mean, just because someone was a celebrity didn't mean they wanted to be adored. Sometimes it was a role assigned to you, not one you sought out.

"Don't bother anyone, but if you should feel inclined, Mrs. Vestum is someone I'd love to meet."

Of course she was. I didn't know if she'd be okay meeting strangers, and we were really busy with the under-cover search for whoever was behind the murders. And training me.

"I'll ask her," I said. "Maybe at the festival, some of the more famous residents could hold a meet-and-greet."

She smiled at me like I'd made her year, then sent me on my way.

MRS. VESTUM REACTED JUST as I expected.

"We are not a tourist attraction."

Unfortunately for her, she radiated pleasure that far outweighed her words.

"Who is 'we'?"

"Leave it, Cossi. I will talk to the others. Perhaps a small set of workshops would be appropriate, but I am not posing for selfies."

I tried really hard not to laugh but it just bubbled out of

me. The idea of her posing for a photo that would be put online just tickled me.

"I'll make tea, and we will go back to work," she said as her shield against my powers slammed into place.

Two hours later, we'd made progress. I had cast and dispersed several useful spells. A cleaning one that would make life owning a B&B infinitely easier. A seeking spell that worked on objects that we thought might be useful if we ever matched a talisman to a witch. And a peace spell. When she mentioned it, I thought she meant something that would stop a fight, but no. It was to create a feeling of peace. Another asset for The Inner Spell.

"I think your spell work training is done," she said. "You are proficient and can focus for the time required. Now you simply need to keep practicing with new ones."

I almost opened my mouth to argue with her. Sure, I could light a flame as long as I knew exactly where the source was. It would help me light candles in the building without actually being there, as long as no one moved them. And I knew how to do multiple seeking and shielding spells, but that didn't seem enough to me.

I had to trust her, right? If she thought I was ready for self-exploration, that meant we could focus on another area. Preferably, the search for whoever was forcing witches to kill — and then suddenly die if they tried to explain what happened.

"The talismans," she said. "Did you draw them as I asked?"

This was a discussion from weeks ago. I'd shown her the photos, but she demanded that I draw them in as much detail as I could. I'd negotiated a delay so I could set up The Inner Spell — and learn how to draw. But my time was up.

"Not all," I said.

"Do you have the ones you completed?" She held out her hand ready if my answer was yes.

It was. I pulled the small drawing pad from my backpack. I'd tried to sketch them from the pictures because I wasn't comfortable carrying the talismans with me. They were far safer in my room under the protection of the spell bag. The thing is, I got a different result when I drew with the original in front of me.

"There are two versions," I said. "I guess three, really. I know I'm not great at drawing and I did my best but, well, you'll see."

She put her phone on the table with the photos open. Then she flipped the pages on my art pad.

"I told you why you needed to make the drawings from the actual stones. It's clear you drew from the photograph. Why?"

I could have tried to make up a story, but she'd know.

"I was really busy, and sitting down in my room drawing a rock with writing on it took too much time."

"So, you were lazy."

"I wouldn't say that, but yes, I tried a shortcut. Before you lecture me, look at the results."

"No lecture. You stumbled on something."

Even those few words of denial gave me the feeling I was being chastised. Maybe it was something inside me. Probably, it was my baggage, if I was honest. I didn't argue, just let her examine the ten sketches.

"Are these in order? You drew first from the photo, then the original?" She looked up at me and I felt a tiny wave of her emotions. She was proud of me.

"Yes. When I noticed the difference, I made sure not to change anything."

"As I suspected, a spell is distorting the way we see these. If we can remove it, I think the owners will be obvious."

Before I could respond, Destroyer spoke in my mind.

"Murder."

6

M rs. V didn't flinch when I passed on his message. "That bird is getting more dramatic as time goes on."

I fully agreed.

"Where and who?" I asked him, speaking aloud so Mrs. V knew at least my half of the conversation.

"Solitary range. In backyard of witch Pink. The strange witch is dead."

There were two strange witches on the island, maybe more if others were hosting family and friends. Ms. Flor and Mr. Light. "Male or female?"

"Male witch. Staying in your home. Come before you are not allowed to look."

"Martin Light," I said. "I have to go."

"Where is the body?"

"Azalea Pink's yard."

"Go. I will think on this spell."

"Do you think it's weird he was killed in her garden? If he doesn't know anyone here and is shy?"

"Yes. Go before Mark decides you're a nuisance."

I put everything in my backpack and headed out for Beulah. Before I started to ride toward the solitary area, I sent a text to Lilibeth, Lance, and D, inviting them to join me.

"COME ON IN," Azalea Pink said as we walked up her front path. "Everyone is in the back. I'll make refreshments in a bit."

The murder scenes in the past hadn't included catering. Azalea Pink was a lovely person and had helped in a previous murder, but why was she being so callous?

"Hello, Ms. Pink," D said before I could ask her about it. "We need our wits about us to investigate the murder, so don't go to any trouble."

"Ah, yes. I see your point. You aren't visitors. But, tea? Would that be appropriate?"

"I'm not sure how long we'll be here," Mark said as he came from the backyard. "Doc Rene is coming, and we need to look for clues."

"Of course," Azalea said with a twist of her wrist. "Perhaps we can visit later. Young witches are all so fascinating."

She seemed a bit more out of touch these days. I'd learned that solitaries didn't mean hermits. They preferred to do research and experimentation. And sure, there were a lot of semi-hermits among them, but some like Azalea were very social.

"Come on back," Mark said.

Azalea waved her hand in permission for us to enter. I tried to read her, but her emotions were all mixed and blended together. Then I caught a whiff of rum. She was drunk.

I followed Mark into the back and saw Martin's body in a

pile of slack limbs in the center of the unkempt lawn. There was blood on his face and shirt. No weapon sticking out of his chest, but clearly, he'd been stabbed.

"Could Mrs. Pink have done this?" Lilibeth asked.

"She's been visiting other solitaries all morning," Mark said. "The body might have arrived any time after around ten AM."

"Arrived?" D asked.

"No blood," Lance said. "Or, not on the ground anyway."

"Is that common? Every dead body moved by the killer?" I asked before remembering I knew about every murder that ever happened. They'd all happened after I'd arrived.

"It's one common thread," Mark said. "Can you ask your animals if anyone saw anything? I could use some help finding a place to start."

Destroyer gave me a few second's warning before landing on my shoulder. I'd managed to pad every jacket so he could use me as a perch without drilling talon holes in my skin.

"Where's Roy?" I asked. Mark's Australian cattle dog should have been sniffing around the garden for trails.

"Ranging a bit wider. He says there's nothing to follow from the body."

"Could one of your bird army have dropped him?" I asked Destroyer. It would explain the way the body looked.

"No. We find killers, not help them." I passed it on to the others. "Also, how would someone instruct us?"

"You said you can understand human talk," I said.

"Only simple stuff so far. I will improve. And not many people know we have that power. I can understand complexity. But others are not as great and powerful as I am."

I kept the bragging to myself when I confirmed the birds would not have participated.

"He's new," Mark said. "I'll have to ask around to get an ID."

Didn't new people have to register somewhere? Or the person who brought witches here for the first time? I could look into that later.

"His name is Martin Light. He's staying in Phillip's spare room." I got a wave of surprise from Mark with that announcement.

"Then I need to speak to Phillip," he said. "Do you think you can wait for Doc Rene and have her send me the initial report? Start your animal army on the search?"

What? This was the point when he usually told us to go home and keep out of his business.

"We can," Lance said into the silence that followed Mark's request. I wasn't the only one blown away by his words.

"I don't want Phillip to hear through the island gossip," Mark added.

"Did you interview Azalea?" Lilibeth asked.

"Not yet." He paused, and it was obvious he was struggling with the concept of working with us. He really wasn't ready to use a team. "Do it carefully. She wasn't here when it happened. When she reported it, she said the yard was empty when she left. A body showed up and she called me right away."

"Do you believe her?" I asked.

He could tell if she was lying, and I didn't know if anyone could block him. I mean, I had no idea if his power just highlighted lies or if it told him people were telling the truth. Like, if he asked me a question that I answered truthfully, but I had an unrelated secret, would he know?

"I checked her alibi," he said. "Not completely, and there's nothing to show when the body appeared. This early in the investigation, I don't discount anyone."

Maybe Doc Rene would find a time for the body dump. "Okay, we'll see if we can eliminate her."

"And I'll enter everything we find out in the case database." D pulled out his phone. "I'll send you a link. Can we all have access?"

Mark swallowed. I'm not sure if it was in fear we'd be able to read things he'd normally classify, or, if I was right about someone controlling him, maybe he'd need to ask for permission.

"I need to think about that," he said. "Just me for now. You can do what you've done before, right?"

He was careful not to say what that was.

As he walked back to his bike, I wondered why I was so eager to be part of the official investigation. It wasn't that long ago I caught Mark reporting to someone behind our backs. I didn't feel a compulsion spell at work, but I had no idea how to recognize one if it was the reason.

7

W hen Mark rode off, Azalea came out onto her back porch. She was wrapped in a large periwinkle shawl over her flowy dress. She looked worried now in contrast to her earlier party mode. I guess whatever she'd been indulging in had worn off. Or she'd cast a sobering spell. I'd learned those existed after Destroyer's unfortunate experience with a tea Mrs. V used.

"I'll go talk to her now," I said. "Destroyer is calling in some rodents to start searching."

"Probably best for them to hold off until the body is moved?" Lance said. "Part of the challenge with tracking right now is the odor of dead witch. Too much of it, so that scent is masking any others."

"He's told them to wait until I give them the go-ahead." I glanced down at Martin Light's body. He'd been on Henbane less than twenty-four hours. Was that important? Had someone else known he was coming and acted on some old grudge? Or was he simply a convenient victim? I didn't like that thought. It was bad enough that someone had caused the death of three people, five if you count the killers. But did we have someone on the island who liked murdering people?

"I'll come with you," D said. "We don't need three people watching the dead body."

Azalea smiled as we approached. "Mark has gone. Is that a good sign? You've figured out who killed this poor man?"

"Why don't we come in and get you warm," D said.

She pulled the shawl tighter. "Tea? That would be nice. You know how the sober-up spell affects a body. It's like you can't get away from the bad feelings of a hangover, just suffer more because you can think straight."

"Whoever created it had a strong sense of balance," D said. "Pain after pleasure no matter what."

We sat at the table in her kitchen with a view of the garden. I faced the window so Azalea didn't have to stare out at the crumpled form. D filled the kettle and got out mugs.

"Do you know who he is?" Azalea asked.

"He's a visitor," I said. "Martin Light. Have you heard of him?"

"No. Who is hosting him? We get a lot of new people. Well, new to all of us, I suppose, but someone invites them. Real strangers don't just wash up on the shore. This time of year, with the festival, we see faces we haven't seen for a year or more. Not all of us are as adventurous as your parents, D. So often traveling around the wider world. And, Cossi, I hear you are filling your delightful business with guests. How exciting."

D put the mug of tea in front of Azalea, and she took a sip. I did the same, a warming mixture of spices and herbs, and something I didn't recognize. My body felt more comfortable, as though every muscle had let out tension.

"Better?" D asked.

"You are a good boy," Azalea said. "Now, where were we?"

"Martin Light?" I prompted.

"No, I've never heard of him. Do you know where he's staying?"

I told her and waited for any flash of emotion, but nothing came. Was that the tea? I'd have to ask D later.

"Ah. Phillip does go off island, so he meets all kinds of witches. I'll express my sympathy when this is all over."

"Was there anything other than the body that seemed unusual?" D asked.

"I didn't notice," she said. "Shall we look?"

"Not yet," I said. "We need Doc Rene to do her thing, and I'll have some squirrels and such do a search first."

"Oh, that's right, your power. Any luck on finding the third one?"

I guess everyone knew about my suppressed power. "Not yet. Mrs. Vestum and I are working on it." Not exactly a lie; we were working on a lot of things.

The doctor came into my view as she entered the garden. "I'll go talk to her now," I said. "Perhaps you should rest? Get your equilibrium back before you take a look around the garden?"

She gave me a broad smile and went toward a door across the room.

"It's weird, right?" D said.

"Almost everything is weird to me," I said. "What in particular?"

He chuckled and put the mugs in the sink. "I guess two things. This Martin Light guy comes here for the first time and is murdered on the first day. And Mark."

"We'll figure it out," I said. "The first one. There will be a reason he came, and one for his murder. Mark? He said he'd let us help, but you're right. I keep expecting him to suddenly decide we should leave it all alone."

Doc Rene was examining Martin's body. She ran her hands over the lifeless form without actually touching him. Kind of like a *Reiki* session.

"She'll find out what killed him this way," Lilibeth whispered. "Broadly. Like if he was shot through a vital organ, it's probably not more complicated. But if he was poisoned, she'll have to find the actual one."

"And time of death?" In the previous cases, I hadn't been there when Doc Rene worked. My imagination went from the usual mundane thing where all kinds of tests needed to be done before anyone could pinpoint the time, all the way to an instant answer like Professor Plum in the library with the rope idea.

"I'll give you an estimate in a minute," Doc Rene said without turning away from the body.

We stood and watched her work. All we could see was her running her hands just an inch away from the body. Not very exciting.

I heard a rustle in the shrubs bordering the lawn. Pairs of eyes stared back at me. Maybe twenty animals waited for their order to start searching. I made a mental note to stock the feeding stations I'd set up around the island. No one abused the stock of food, which surprised me because I remember epic battles in my old home trying to keep squirrels from the bird feeder.

"Okay. We need to... I guess unfold him and turn him over," Doc Rene said. "He's been stabbed, and the wound must be underneath him. He was tossed from something like a cart. If he was dropped from a height, the bones would be broken."

D and Lance gently unfolded Martin's body.

"No rigor?" I asked.

Doc Rene looked at me. "Too early for it to fully set in. Your time of death is no earlier than five hours ago. I'll know more when I've had some time to analyze the findings."

"Ready," D said. "There's something under him, but I don't want to pull it out before you've done your thing."

I joined them at the body, and we gently placed Martin on his right side. The something was a gold chain.

"There's the wound," Doc Rene said, pointing to his lower back. "One stab, so someone knew what they were doing. Killed elsewhere given the lack of blood and weapon. I need him back at the clinic. The cart is out front."

D and Lance took Martin to the transport. Doc Rene followed them after saying she'd update Mark when her investigation was done.

The gold chain carried a pendant. About the size of an egg, but not as round. Lilibeth put on a pair of latex gloves, and I took out an evidence bag.

"Camera?" she asked.

I put the bag on the ground and took pictures of the jewelry without moving it. "Can you see how it opens?"

Lilibeth picked it up by the pendant. "No catch or anything, but listen." She gave it a gentle shake, holding the chain to prove the rattle we heard was from inside.

"I guess we should leave it to Mark?" I could hear the reluctance in my voice.

"If we want to keep working with him," D said, leaning over to look at the evidence.

"Take pictures for us, just in case Mark reverts to his usual pattern of behavior." Lance sniffed the chain and pendant. "His scent. Someone else, but it's very faint."

8

We decided to let Mark do his thing until we had a chance to absorb what we knew.

And that pendant needed to be opened.

Doc Rene needed time to identify any clues on the body, and my animal team was sniffing out a trail or anything that would lead us to where Martin was killed, or to the killer. I was getting tired of the whole moving the body thing. It used up some of our precious time, but eventually we always found evidence that led us to the killer. I mean, it's a small island, so the search could only take so long.

"We can't figure it out from the photos," D said. "Opening the pendant, I mean. Mrs. V will have a solution, I'm sure."

She was the island's crime lab. The pendant in its bag was sitting on her kitchen table, thanks to a swallow who flew it to her.

"I should check on my guest," I said. "I don't want her getting worried that strangers are dying."

I sent a text to Ms. Flor asking if she needed any assistance finding a place to eat.

She responded that she was at The Howling Place and would find her way back to The Inner Spell. It seemed she wasn't shy, like our victim, and well able to entertain herself.

"Meet for breakfast?" D asked. "At Jan's?"

That would give me time to organize my thoughts and continue my education. Mrs. V had just assigned me three large books to study.

I ARRIVED home and Mark was still with Phillip in the kitchen.

"You've heard?" Phillip asked me. He was experiencing grief. I felt it souring his general emotions. I had no idea if it was the right amount, but we all feel loss in our own ways.

"Cossi is going to help me find the killer," Mark said. Making it official so he couldn't back out?

"I see," Phillip said. "Well, you know what's the best course of action. I think I'll retire. If you need to search Martin's room, do it now, please. Then perhaps you can leave me in peace for a while."

When he left, Mark started putting his notes away. He pulled out a pair of gloves and his camera. "Want to join me?"

The answer was yes. But I didn't say anything because I felt like I was doing something wrong. Martin would hate the idea of someone snooping in his room.

"He's gone, Cossi. I don't think the guy would want us to ignore something that finds his killer."

Was I that transparent?

He handed me gloves, and we walked to the end of the hall where Martin spent his last night alive.

At the door, Mark stepped inside. I couldn't move.

"I'm stuck," I said.

"Spell bag, or a spell on the door to keep you out? Maybe you and Phillip?" Mark said.

"I can see why he'd want to stop us snooping," I said. "You aren't affected?"

"He didn't expect other witches to try, I guess. I'll do the search. If I find a bag, I can remove it. If it's a spell, we'll need one of the elders to deal with it."

Because there were rules? "Can't you undo it? You're the cop, surely no one can keep you out."

He held out his arms to prove he was free to move. "I'm not being kept out, Cossi. The elders know more about this stuff, and it's faster to get them to deal with it."

I moved back, glad the spell let me go anywhere but closer to the doorway.

Phillip joined us at that moment. "Oh, is something wrong?"

Mark called him over and asked him to try entering the room. He got stuck in exactly the same place I did.

"I'll call Mrs. Vestum," Phillip said.

"No. I'd like to leave it in place until the case is over," Mark said. "Saves me from locking it off."

Phillip nodded and went through the door leading to the bookstore.

"Do you want me to watch?" I asked.

"No. I'm sure you have better things to do than that," he said. His phone buzzed with an incoming text. He looked at it and grunted. "You know, maybe I should get Mrs. V to remove the spell first. I can put an official block on right away."

Was that because of the text? I didn't ask because being nosy like that could get us kicked off the investigation. "Okay, so what do we do now?"

"I'll go talk to Doc Rene," he said. "We need her results to decide where to go next."

When Mark left, I headed back to my room. The reading assignment still needed doing, and those talismans were calling me.

___

9

My phone pinged with a text notice an hour later.

It was far too soon for Mark to have answers.

I looked and it was from Mrs. V. Not a demand to know how much reading I'd accomplished; she'd done that for the first few days of our new relationship. The council was meeting, and my presence was required.

I knew for sure this wasn't a regular meeting, so I couldn't help worry about what I'd done now.

The meeting was in the business building at the wharf end of the street, so only a minute before I was sitting on the chair facing eight of the nine council members. D's dad was still absent, and this time he hadn't sent D along with voting instructions.

"The question has arisen about your involvement in the current investigation," Mr. Macy said. "Your plate is full, Cossi. We are concerned your studies or your business will suffer if you continue to assist Mark in his duties."

Was this coming from Mrs. V? I didn't think she'd go

behind my back. She was too comfortable confronting me face to face.

"What do you have to say to that?" Phillip asked.

"I didn't realize you'd asked a question," I said. "I think Mark should be the one to decide if he needs help."

I was not going to throw him under the bus by saying he wasn't capable of solving the latest murder.

"We are prepared to give him assistance," Phillip said. "There are police in other communities."

"My business doesn't take much of my time," I said. "I'm fully booked until after the festival. I need to arrange for breakfast and dinner when more guests arrive. My current guest is more than happy to explore the opportunities Henbane offers."

"Sounds under control to me," Jeffery Peak said. He'd become more of an advocate for me since his own misadventures in the last case."

"Your studies?" Dolph asked.

He raised an eyebrow at me. His emotions were in check, so I had no idea if he was giving me a hint on how to answer, or expressing surprise I wasn't overwhelmed.

"I think I have managed to balance learning with everything else I have to do," I said. "Mrs. Vestum is more qualified than I am to answer you."

If she was behind this, I'd given her the opening she needed.

"Cossi has a long way to go," she said. "Her progress is acceptable at this point. I imagine we will accelerate the demand on her time as she gains more knowledge."

Two of the other councilors exchanged comments. Ashley Ivers, our accountant, and Effie Walsh, our grocer, looked at me and smiled.

"It is dangerous," Phillip said, "for an untrained witch to dig into the secrets we all hold."

"I think it is time for us to vote on this subject," Jeffery Peak said. "We have the power to order Cossi off the investigation. If we are tied, I will use my extra vote so we don't need to disturb Batiste Rothtect. All who wish her to cease investigating, please vote now."

I held my breath.

One hand went up. Phillip.

"All who wish her to continue?" Jeffery asked.

Seven hands shot up. They were all anxious to get back to their own work.

"Then the meeting is adjourned." Jeffery stood and took his leather jacket off the back of his chair.

"Cossi, I was just thinking of your safety," Phillip said as he passed me.

10

A fter the council meeting, I was so wound up I'd only gotten a couple of hours' sleep. Was I supposed to tell Mark about the meeting? Did I care? He needed to know Phillip had tried to get me off the case, so yes. And Mrs. Vestum? Why hadn't she given me a heads-up?

The only benefit of losing a night's sleep was how much I got ahead in my reading. And that I was awake to get Ms. Flor's text. She didn't need breakfast and would be back at her chalet later in the day in case I was worried. She didn't say she'd hooked up with a shifter from The Howling Place, but her emoji use was hard to ignore. A wolf, a heart and an eggplant. Good for her.

I headed over to Jan's for our morning update meeting.

Mark was at the table with the others, which I took as a good sign. I decided to get it over with and told them about the meeting last night while we waited for Jan to deliver our orders.

"I didn't complain, Cossi," Mark said. He looked around

the table. "I know I've been an idiot in the past, but none of you had any history of investigations. And you were completely new. I mean, everyone was new to investigating, and you were new to this entire way of living."

I touched his arm. "I didn't think it came from you. Let's be honest, though. You were just as inexperienced at murder investigations as any one of us."

"Thanks, I guess," he said. "Anyway, we need to talk about what we know. I have to say it feels good to have a sounding board."

"We have a bunch of things we're waiting for," D said.

Jan interrupted to place breakfast on the table. "How's Phillip taking the death of his friend?"

I couldn't say what I thought, that he was being a pain over it, because it might be how he was processing his feelings.

"Hard," I said. "I think he's trying to protect people now. Trying to control everything."

"You'll find the reason and the killer," Jan said. "I'll bring over the pot of coffee so you can talk without me butting in with great service."

"Two things outstanding," Mark said. "Doc Rene's report. I'm hoping that will give us some direction, and opening that pendant."

"And any results from Cossi's search team," Lilibeth asked.

"What about motive?" Lance asked.

"Yes, we need to find that," Mark said. "I meant two things I hoped would be answered today. It's going to take me a while to get used to teamwork."

He wasn't the only one. I had those talismans. Maybe if I showed them around, someone would know who owned them. Mrs. V was the only one I'd talked to about the stones and markings. I had reason, not because I wanted to keep secrets, but because I'd been so busy. And if I was completely honest with myself, I wanted to be the one who found all the answers to their secrets.

It was only a few steps from Jan's to home, so I could just grab them after we'd finished with the rest of the update.

"Did Mrs. Vestum have any ideas?" D asked. "On the pendant."

Mark nodded and pulled out his notebook. "She isn't able to open it, but she's heard of these things. There will be a spell or a specific touch pattern that will make it open. She'll do what she can to test some spells. Do we know if he brought it with him?"

The question was directed at me. "I have no idea. I only saw him for a few minutes. He said hello and then went to his room. Maybe Phillip will know?"

"Leave that to me," Mark said. "If Phillip is unhappy with you working on the case, it's probably better that you don't interview him."

"Good point." I didn't want to push his buttons any more than I had to. He'd seemed so nice at the beginning, but in light of him calling the council together to stop me investigating, I wondered if he had a spiteful side.

"Why did he come?" Lilibeth asked. "I thought he didn't know anyone here. And the festival isn't something a really shy person would enjoy."

Something niggled at the back of my mind, but I couldn't quite pin it down. "I think he was looking for something to do with his research," I said. "He didn't say, and Phillip didn't tell me, but if not for the festival, why now?"

"And why would someone kill him?" D asked. "If he

hadn't been here before. What could he have done or seen that someone needed him dead?"

Lots of questions, but with him dead, we might not get any answers. "When will Doc Rene be finished?" I changed the subject to stop the spiral of 'I don't knows'.

"She said she'd have something for us in a couple of hours," Mark said. "But she said he was definitely dead before he was put in the garden. It wasn't a drop, but more like he was rolled along the path. He died and lay on his back for at least an hour before being moved."

"That stab wound would leave a lot of blood, wherever it happened." Lance waved for a coffee refill. "Anything from the animals?"

"Not yet. The handover to the nocturnal animals was a bit ragged because there's not usually much overlap. I haven't heard from Destroyer yet. I'll reach out when we're done here."

"There was someone's scent on the pendant," Lance said. "I'll wander around to see if I can pick it up."

"You didn't recognize it?" Mark asked. "Maybe the killer is from the mainland."

"I don't know," Lance said. "It's that feeling like you know the answer but can't access it. So, it had the feeling of familiarity, but I can't figure out why. We could send a few other shifters to try."

"I'll talk to Mrs. V," Mark said. "That's a good idea. The more people aware of the problem, the more likely we are to get an answer."

I desperately tried to erase the image of a crowd of shifters sniffing everyone they came into contact with.

"I have something else," I said. "I don't know if it has anything to do with this case, but it might help us find whoever is making it happen. All the deaths."

"We need to focus on the murder in front of us," Mark said.

"We have nothing to follow up on just yet," I said. "I'll be back in a minute. Don't do anything interesting until I get back."

11

———

When I returned with the bag full of talismans, Mark was standing outside Jan's on the phone. It reminded me of the same thing happening a few days ago. When he'd taken the call and mentioned my name. I'd decided then not to give him my full trust. And here I was about to show him the talismans. Why? I hadn't made a decision to trust him. I did it automatically.

I couldn't back out now, but I would remind myself in the future to think before I handed him information I didn't need to share.

"I told you I wouldn't do that," Mark said. He ended the call as I walked up.

"Problem?" I asked.

"I'm handling it," he said. "Let's get back inside."

We rejoined the others, and I put the bag on the table without opening it.

"Many trails," Destroyer said in my mind.

"Anything useful?" I asked. Then mouthed 'Destroyer' to my friends.

"Some," he said. "We will explore."

"Also, the witch wasn't killed there," I said.

"Look again for a place with lots of blood?"

"I think so, but as soon as I know anything more, I'll tell you."

"Roy is with us," he said. "When we capture the killer, we will call for you."

He said it like we hadn't been involved in capturing the last murderers. "Don't wait that long."

I took a sip of my coffee. Jan had warmed it up while I was gone. I passed on Destroyer's news and then touched the bag. "These were buried in a box up at The Inner Spell."

Mark reached for the bag, but I pulled it away. I wanted to talk about the talismans before I showed them.

"Mrs. Vestum agrees these are talismans, and there are fifteen." I waited to see if anyone made the connection with what Carly told us before she died.

"The same number as the names on the list," Lance said. "We should be able to identify the witches by their talismans."

"Would a shifter have one?" I asked.

"As a gift," D said. "It wouldn't mean the same for a shifter as it would for a witch. Not just jewelry, but more a protective spell or something like that. For a witch, a talisman is a powerful object."

"Do they have symbols on them?" Mark asked. "We should be able to identify the witches by the symbols. If they match the victims and murderers so far, we will know who was on the list."

I closed my eyes and tried to quiet the frustrated voice inside that said we'd tried, but as usual, nothing was easy.

"So, here's the thing," I said. "I took photos of them and showed them to Mrs. V. She told me to draw them. I'm not an artist, so it's taking a while for me to get them right."

"I can try," Lilibeth said. "I sketch all the time."

That was good news because I had a plan.

"I want all of you to try to draw the one I take out. I'm not going to tell you anything until we see what you come up with."

They grabbed pencils and paper from their packs and waited. No one argued, and for that I was grateful. The experiment would only work if they went in without preconceptions.

I reached in and pulled out the first one that came to hand. I placed it on the table, symbol side up. It was one I'd tried to draw. Good, another point of comparison.

Four pencils moved on the paper, and it only took minutes to see that I was right.

"That's not what it looks like," Lance said, glancing at Lilibeth's work.

"It is," she said. "You're the one who has it wrong."

"You've all drawn something different," I said. "I did too. Something is muddling our perception."

Around the table were sketches with slight similarities, but significantly different end results. Most had the shape more or less correct, but some were more jagged, and some more square. The symbols were nothing alike.

"A spell," Mark said. "We'll never be able to match these to witches."

"Mrs. V will figure it out," I said. "Take a photo of your drawings, please."

The same thing happened this time. The photos of the sketches were right, but when I asked them to snap a picture of the stone, another four different objects showed up. Maybe all the pictures and sketches would tell Mrs. V something.

"Send them to her, and I'll text her why," I said. "I think

these will unlock the answer to the whole picture, but right now, as Mark said, we have a murder to solve."

"It's weird," D said. "Knowing that those talismans must belong to people we know. People who might be killers."

"Or not," Mark said. "Until we know exactly what they are, we can't rely on them being connected."

Knowing he had a point didn't stop me from believing the talismans held the secret to all the problems. Why witches and shifters were dying. Who was behind the whole thing, and if my mother started it all.

"Inside a house," Destroyer said in my mind. It had the feeling of a half-conversation. Like I'd been ignoring him.

I held up a hand to quiet the others. "Destroyer just checked in." When they acknowledged me, I focused on my familiar. "What did you say? I missed something."

"Mouse said dead witch was in a house. Not where he was found. Other solitary."

I passed on the message.

"Who?" Mark asked. He was already putting his things away in preparation to start the investigation again."

"I heard," Destroyer said.

"You can hear other people through my mind?" Creepy.

"No. You thought his word."

Something to remember as we learned more about this relationship.

"Do you have an answer?"

"Don't know name. Near the garden he was found. Come to there and I will show you."

I passed it along to the others, and we headed out to Azalea Pink's house.

12

_____

It turned out I knew the solitary whose house smelled like Martin Light. We'd talked when Jeffery Peak went missing. Lawson Quisk was a friend of Azalea's, but that didn't mean much. In the world of solitaries, being best friends didn't mean you knew much about each other.

We must have looked a bit intimidating when he opened his door. Five of us crowded on his front porch, with Destroyer on my shoulder. His eyes widened, and for a second I felt fear. Then he smiled.

"What brings you to my door?" he asked, opening it wider. "Please come in. I'll make tea. It's a little early for anything stronger. Isn't it?"

The last was said in a tone that invited us to disagree. My last encounter with him had involved morning drinking.

"Tea will be fine," Mark said. "We need to talk to you about Martin Light. The witch found in Ms. Pink's garden yesterday."

Lawson turned from the stove where he'd lit the element under a large kettle. "Ms. Pink? Oh, Azi. Yes, I heard we had another murder. What is this island coming to? Sit. I'll find a few cookies to go along with our tea."

I was happy to let Mark do the talking. It left me free to read the emotions Lawson was making no effort to hide. He was curious and sad. His absent-mindedness was real. I guess living mostly alone made it hard to keep connected to the larger world.

We waited until he'd made the tea, something with herbs and lemon, and joined us at his table. We were squished on the banquette, which was made to hold three people. Mark and Lance perched on the very edge.

"The mouse was right," Lance whispered, "but Lawson is not the witch I scented on the body."

Lawson placed a cooled saucer of tea on the floor. "Your familiar, if he wants. I have nothing more appropriate for a crow. I am sorry."

"Kind of you to think of him," I said. I turned to Mark, hoping he'd start the interview. Being scrunched in like this was the most uncomfortable I'd been in a long time. I'd be happy when we were done.

"Did you know Mr. Light?" Mark asked as he put his notebook on the table beside his phone. "I'm sure you don't mind me recording this interview."

"Record away. I can never remember what I've agreed to do during conversations. Perhaps you can set me up with some similar device, Didier?"

D agreed to teach him and then looked at Mark. I wasn't the only one hoping to move this along. Especially since Lance had confirmed the mouse had found Martin's presence, and that another scent was on the body.

"Mr. Light?" Mark prompted. "Did you know him?"

"It depends on what you mean by know," Lawson said. "I was aware of him. I suppose I did know him to some extent."

Phillip told me Martin was a stranger to the island.

"I need you to explain," Mark said.

"Ah, yes. So, Martin and a few others around here were part of an online group exploring the idea of integrating more with the mundane world. The communities on the mainland and around the world in urban centers are finding it increasingly difficult to remain hidden. Not as hidden as we are, of course. But undetected is probably more accurate."

They should have asked me. I could tell them it would be a disaster if they were discovered. But then, the witches living away from Henbane would have known it all too well.

"That couldn't have been popular," Mark said. "Can you tell me who on the island was part of the group?"

"I can do better," he said. "I'll invite you to join and you can see the names. No one is using a false identity. Well, as far as I know. I mean, we don't do that video stuff, so I suppose someone could be pretending."

"I can work that out," Mark said. "As far as we knew, Mr. Light didn't have any contacts other than Phillip Raziel on the island."

"I suppose that is true, in a way," Lawson said. He took one of the lemon cookies and dipped it in his tea while he thought. "Oh blast," he said as the cookie disintegrated into the mug.

"Did anyone in the group disagree with the idea?" Mark asked.

"We hadn't gotten that far," Lawson said. "Nothing would be published until we had some solid findings, of course. Too easy to start a panic. And without data, people would have nothing to argue against."

"The idea," I said. "Just thinking about exposing magic might frighten people."

"True, and we here on Henbane are not the best judges. I fear that the witches and others who live in the world may not have a choice."

"Please send me the invitation now," Mark said, "so you don't need to worry about it later."

"Of course. Let me get my laptop." He wandered off to a side room.

"I can research the members of the group," D said. "But like he said, Henbane isn't impacted by this, so why would anyone here kill to stop it? And would they stop working because one member is killed?"

"We won't have any answers until we have the names," Mark said. "Cossi, ask Mrs. V if she knows anything about this."

I sent a text. "She might not answer right away." If she didn't know, what would happen? As the protector of the paranormal world, this was her authority. Or it should be.

My phone pinged.

"She gave them permission to form. They are supposed to report to her. She doesn't know who belongs to the group. Lawson is her contact."

Relief came at me from all sides. Except from me. I could only wonder why she hadn't mentioned it, since I had a point of view that no one else on the island did. And she said she didn't know Martin. Would she really have given them the go-ahead and then stepped away?

Mark's phone buzzed and he looked at the screen. His face hardened and he swiped to ignore the call, then rubbed his temples like he had a headache.

"I sent you the email," Lawson said as he rejoined us. "I have been thinking on what you said. We didn't know Martin was coming to Henbane early. I had no idea Phillip knew him, and it's not because of this group. We'd decided to keep the members secret, even from Mrs. V." His eyes widened, and a flash of fear hit me. "Are we all targets?"

"I don't think so, but keep alert, and set some strong wards. Is there anything else that might help us find the killer?" Mark asked. I thought that was a very broad question given Lawson's rambling.

"We were supposed to meet in person at the festival," he said. "Other witches are coming for the festival now that you have created accommodation, Cossi. I was looking forward to seeing the faces behind the discussion. Oh, and not only committee members. I'm pretty certain I saw Tony Reed when I went into Effie's for supplies. And the Alders have a couple of guests."

13

M ark sent D the list of members in the group when we were back on the road. We stood by our bikes because no one knew what to do. I mean, we had an earful of information now, but nothing we could act on right away.

"I will continue to direct the searchers," Destroyer said before he flew off.

"D, do the research on those names," Mark said. "Lilibeth, can you go talk to Doc Rene to see if she needs help? And Lance, I think it's time to bring the shifters into this. They can travel much faster than mice and squirrels."

He'd learned fast. Going from working alone to delegating tasks was a huge leap.

"What do I do?" I still needed to do some classes with Mrs. V.

"What do you know about your guest?" Mark asked.

"Ms. Flor? I can check in on her, but she's enjoying the island and seems to be happy to be left alone."

"Send D her details," Mark said. "We might need to talk

to her. If these group members are converging on us, I'd need to investigate any off-islanders, even without a murder."

I sent D a text with the names of all my guests. "Done. Now what? Is there a register that will tell us who'd come to stay with friends or relatives?"

"No. I want to search Martin Light's room again. Now we have more information."

"I can't help with that because of the spell."

"I need to stop at Sweet and Bitter," he said. "Mr. Macy will have something we can use to cancel the spell temporarily."

I CHECKED out the shelves of teas and potions in Mr. Macy's shop. I needed to talk to him about setting up a booth at the festival. If I was going to have one, I could give space for some of the local people. Not as competition for their own booths, but as an added source of clients.

He'd also offered to lead me on a mind-bending trip to find my last power. Shrooms or something else. I didn't know the cultural issues, or really like the idea of losing control. Accepting his offer was at the bottom of my to-do list and might stay there forever.

"Cossi, let's go," Mark said as he touched my elbow. I guess I'd been deep into my thoughts because his words came with a tone of 'can you hear me'.

I nodded at the paper sack he carried. "That's it?"

"Yes. A little something for the doorway, and for you. We'll be able to search for an hour or so before the spell starts pushing you out."

I didn't want to know what that might feel like. I guessed

anything from a gentle push back into the hall, to a sudden need to use the toilet.

Phillip was in the bookstore on the phone when we walked through to the stairs leading to the apartment. We could have gone around the side, but Mark wanted to make sure Phillip knew we were going up.

The 'something for the doorway' turned out to be burning sage and lavender and sending the smoke through to the bedroom. The 'something for me' was a shower of water that smelled like Earl Grey tea. Mark flicked it from a fir branch.

"Go ahead," he said and nodded toward the room.

I didn't feel any magic. Two steps past the door, I turned around. Nothing had even required effort. "Let's do this."

The room was more like a double-wide closet. A single bed with a night table holding a lamp. Three tiny drawers in the nightstand and a dresser against the wall didn't leave much space to hide secrets.

"Check the drawers," Mark said. "I'll do the dresser. If we don't find anything, I'll move the bed so you can look underneath."

"We should check the mattress, too," I said. "I can fix whatever mess we make before we leave."

I mean, it couldn't take more than twenty minutes to uncover anything Martin might have hidden.

Mark opened the first drawer. "Pull them out," he said, demonstrating. "If the object is small enough, it could be taped under it, or on the backboard."

"We'll need to remove the spell," I said as I pulled out all three of the night table drawers. It's not going to be great for Phillip if no one can come in."

Mark grunted in agreement — or maybe something else.

My power was damped down. I hadn't realized until I tried to check his emotions.

"What did that water do to me?" I dumped out a pile of papers from the bottom drawer.

"Muffled you. So it's like you're not here. The smoke dulled whatever spell protected the place, and with you being minimized, it can't tell you're here."

"Okay, just to let you know, I don't like it." The papers had nothing to do with Martin. Some receipts from five years ago for book purchases, and a couple of old grocery lists. This was stuff from Phillip using the room as an office.

"No one does," he said. "Nothing in or on the dresser."

I turned over the final drawer after checking the back. Nothing. I pulled the table away from the wall. A slim leather-bound book was held on the back of the night table with packing tape. "Check this out."

Mark stood beside me, and we both stared at the book. Something tickled across my shoulders, like a spider had run across my skin. I asked who was here in my head, but no animal or other creature answered. It could be that no one was here, or the spell might be locking down my language power.

He dug an evidence bag from his pocket. "Hold this."

I took it and opened the top as wide as I could.

He peeled the tape off the wood and put the whole thing in the bag.

"Aren't we going to look inside?" If he was about to pull his usual 'kicking me off the case as soon as we had a lead', I would... What? I couldn't run anywhere.

Another spider ran across my skin. I brushed at my shoulders. I guess just because I asked if anyone was in the room, it didn't mean they had to answer me.

"How are you feeling?" Mark took the bag but didn't seal it.

"Fine," I said automatically. Then something crawled up my leg. "What the heck?"

"I told you the spell would make you leave," he said with a laugh. "Martin could have made it far more aggressive."

I ran for the door, trying not to rub all the imaginary bugs off my skin.

14

A s soon as I stood on the other side of Martin's door, the feelings disappeared, so I was laughing with Mark after a few minutes. I wondered if that was Martin's doing. Or if whoever made the spell had the sense of humor of an eight-year-old.

"I'll ask Mrs. V to find the security spell and deactivate it as soon as we don't need it for the investigation."

"You think there's more in that tiny space?" I couldn't see where he'd managed to hide something else we couldn't have found in five minutes.

"I think it's dangerous to let anyone walk in and plant something," he said.

Mrs. V opened the door before he could knock. I'd thought it was some kind of power she had that let her know when people approached. I guess it was, but not the kind of power like talking to animals. She told me she'd had a ward spell set on the path to her door when I asked.

Mark held out the unsealed evidence bag. "Diary," he said, "from Martin Light's room."

She beckoned us in and told him to put the bag on the table. "I've seen the drawings," she said.

It took me a moment to remember what we'd done that morning. "The talismans? Did it help?"

"I'll need to look at the actual objects," she said. "Bring them when you come for your next lesson."

"Shouldn't we be looking at the book?" Mark asked.

"Tea first," Mrs. V said.

"I have the talismans with me now," I said. Sure, Mark was right. The murder should take precedence, but if we could figure out these mysterious objects, I knew we'd have the entire answer. Or, one step in that direction.

"Put them with the book," she said. "We have time for both."

How could she be so sure? I pulled the bag of talismans from my backpack and put them next to the evidence bag.

"It turns out Martin Light had a few acquaintances," Mark said. "I don't know if Phillip was lying or if Martin lied to him."

Speaking of lies. "Mrs. V, why didn't you tell me about the committee?"

She didn't turn me into a toad, so I guess it was a good question?

"I didn't see it as important enough to interrupt your lessons," she said.

I bit back the 'well, it seems like you were wrong' because it wouldn't get me anywhere but more lessons.

"Take care accusing Phillip Raziel," Mrs. V said to Mark. "You know he can take offense when it's not offered."

So, I was right that he'd been mad at me for taking a new mentor.

"I can't let hurt feelings get in the way of the truth."

Mark accepted the teacup and then put his notebook and phone on the table. "The book?"

Mrs. Vestum gave him a needling glare. I'd been on the receiving end of it enough times to be impressed by the way he ignored it.

She grunted acceptance of his point. I wondered what he thought the sound meant. I only knew because the emotion flowed to me.

"Cossi, drink your tea while I look at this diary. Perhaps Martin Light wrote that he was about to be murdered and named the killer."

Mark and I watched as she slipped on some cotton gloves and reached into the bag. She started by placing her hand on the cover and closing her eyes. I'd learned enough to know that she was searching for any trace of magic. Opening the book could trigger a booby trap that destroyed everything.

"There is a protection," she said. "I need to study it a little more. Leave it with me and I will inform you of any details related to your case."

I expected Mark to push or tell her he couldn't leave the book with a civilian. Fortunately, before I made a fool of myself, I remembered that she was his crime lab.

"Names would be nice," I said, "but I guess the animals might come up with something."

"Now," Mrs. V said, drawing the bag of talismans toward her. "Let's see what surprises await us in here."

Given that they seemed capable of generating illusions, I half expected the items to fall out as acorns, or leaves, or something other than the lumps of stone I saw when I looked at them.

Nope, there they were, fifteen lumps of stone with runes on them.

"Cossi, did you not feel the magic imbued here?" Mrs. V asked. "Layers of it."

Another thing I was supposed to know.

"They felt slippery," I said. "Not physically, but I guess that was the magic?"

"Everyone feels it differently," Mark said. "So that's why no one can really pin down what they look like?"

"The spell is part of it," she said. "Leave these with me also. I need to identify the components before I dig into the actual spell. Whoever did this is powerful. Not many people are able to use this much magic and still be subtle."

"Do you know who they are?" I asked. "We could start with a list of names."

She poured the stones into the bag and pulled the drawstring. "I know most of the witches capable of this. I didn't feel anything familiar, so I will not provide names until I know more. If I am wrong, we risk warning the person behind everything."

Mark made a note in his book and put his phone away. "We can't trust what we see right now," he said. "I mean, we know that because we all see a different thing. But a witch with this much power is also capable of masking their abilities. It could be a witch that no one suspects is powerful."

Why did everything get more complicated? "So, we're kind of stuck until Mrs. V can dive into two different magical problems. What do we do now?"

"The murder investigation. You never needed my help before, Cossi. Why don't you have a plan?" He stood and then pulled out his phone. The screen was lit up with a call and I saw Phillip's name. He ignored it.

"The solitaries?" I said. I couldn't quite trust Mark, but if Phillip was calling, it meant something. "That's what we'd do. Talk to more of them. And we need to follow up with D about the members of the group Lawson told you about."

"And see if Lilibeth and Doc Rene found any clues," Mark added. "And Lance. Perhaps the shifters found a lead."

"Okay it seems like we're not at a standstill," I said.

Mark's phone buzzed with a text notification.

"First, we need to update Phillip," he said.

"Is that normal? For you to update a person of interest?"

"Is he a suspect?" Mrs. V asked. "That's going to complicate things. He's Mark's council representative."

"So, the answer is yes," Mark said. "It's normal for me to keep him updated. And no, I'm not convinced he's involved in this murder."

15

I gave Mark the opportunity to meet Phillip alone. Sure, I didn't want to be there because it might become a thing Phillip could use against me for... I don't know what. But I liked thinking it was for Mark and not for me. He told me I needed to be there — so much for wishful thinking.

"He knows you're working the case," Mark said. "Remember, he's my representative on council."

"I didn't think you could be fired," I said. Mark was supposed to be the cop based on his powers.

"He can make things harder," Mark said, "but he'd need the council behind him to take my job. And that's unlikely, given the murders."

A weird mixture of relief and fear followed his words.

"Okay. I'll keep quiet, though. That's the best, right?" *Please say yes.*

"I know how to give him an update," Mark said. "So, unless he asks you something directly, you can just listen."

We walked up Main Street to the bookstore. "Who

would do the job if you didn't? And what would you do instead?"

It was the nerves talking. I still had to live in the apartment above the store. Moving into one of the rooms up at The Inner Spell was looking more like a good option — not today, but soon.

"They aren't going to fire me," he said, "but Dolph would want one of the shifters, and Mrs. V wouldn't let anyone but a witch do the job. Maybe a shifter like Lance and a witch like you as partners would be acceptable."

"I don't want the job," I said. "And what would you do if you weren't the island police? And what about Roy? Would you just hand him off to the next cop?"

"A vacation to start with," he said. "Maybe a cop in another community. Roy will be fine. Stop asking questions, we need to focus."

Phillip was waiting in the bookstore.

"My friend needs justice," Phillip said. "This affects the island as a whole. What have you found?"

No hi. No good to see you. This was a completely different side to Phillip. Sure, he wasn't all warm and cuddly, but never rude — until now.

"The investigation is moving along," Mark said. "I can't give you a lot of specifics because the leads are complicated. We will find whoever killed your friend."

"Why can't you trust me with the information?"

He seemed genuinely hurt. At least, that was the vibe I got. But maybe Mark could read something like a lie. Now I wanted to know if his lie detector power was subtle enough to know if someone was just pretending. The questions in my head just kept growing. One answer seemed to spawn ten new gaps in my understanding of my home.

"You know how rumors get started," Mark said. "It's like

we can all read minds when it comes to winkling out juicy secrets. The last thing we want is to tip off the killer."

"Hmm. True," Phillip said. "Do you have any idea why he was found in Azalea's garden? Is she a suspect?"

He wasn't going to accept that Mark wouldn't tell him the details. I pressed my lips together because the words were trying to leap out of my mouth. I started telling myself over and over to let Mark run the meeting — like a mantra.

"Cossi," Phillip said. "You met Martin, and I'm sure you're with me that the case will be more easily solved with more input."

My mantra changed to 'don't ask me'.

"We're all working toward finding the killer," I said, carefully skirting the real question. Would I actually need to stay out at The Inner Spell until we solved the case? Living here would give Phillip the opportunity to keep pushing.

Instead of demanding an answer, he sighed. "I suppose you are right," he said, to my relief. "I will step back as I usually do. I would appreciate it if you gave me a heads-up before the entire island knows who killed Martin."

"Can you answer a few questions while we're here?" Mark asked. "You probably knew him best. Is there a particular reason he came this year?"

We hadn't dug into the list of people in the research group Lawson mentioned. If Phillip was one of them, he would be a good source of leads.

"He told me it was just interest in a society that didn't need to deal with non-magical humans. I did tell him that's not Henbane; we still need the regular world to provide us with a multitude of items."

"Did he say anything else about it?" Mark asked.

I could feel Phillip struggling to stop from showing his annoyance at the questioning. He didn't want to tell Mark something but couldn't decline to answer the questions after trying to become part of the investigation.

"As far as I know, he didn't have any other contacts here," Phillip said.

I knew that for a lie, and by Mark's sudden stillness, his power caught it too. I knew better than to assume it was from Phillip because Martin could have told him he didn't know anyone.

"Do you know anything about a group set up to study options to integrate better with non-magical people?" Mark wasn't going to give Phillip any information about them if he didn't know. Mrs. V must have had a reason to keep the whole thing secret; we would honor that, I guess.

"I have not, and I would strongly object to taking the risk." He looked at me like it was my idea. "We have past experience with this nonsense to guide us. Are you saying Martin came here to meet with this group? That Henbane residents are putting the island at risk again?"

Wow, that hurt. He was my parents' friend, at least that's what he told me.

"I'm not saying anything," Mark said. "It's a lead, but not the most important. Why do you think the victim didn't know anyone on Henbane?"

Phillip stopped glaring at me and picked up a leather-bound book from the counter. I could feel him taking control of his emotions. If shielding from me was a matter of willpower, his anger had undermined that control. His emotions leaked out of him, full of vibrant color. After a few moments of reading the spine and the copyright page, he regained his balance and sighed.

"He told me at the conference where we met. When he learned I was from Henbane, he said he'd wanted to visit for a long time. I suppose I assumed he didn't have anyone to stay with, so I suggested he take my spare room for the festival. This was before Cossi arrived."

Mark didn't challenge him on any of his statements. "This helps," he said. "More information is always useful in an investigation. Helps to learn when people are holding something back. As usual, when I have a real suspect, I'll update you."

"Be sure you do," Phillip said. "Cossi, I will be out for dinner this evening."

I hadn't planned on coming home for dinner, but I just nodded. I would need to check on my guest at some point today. Maybe she'd like to join me for a picnic dinner out at The Inner Spell. It wasn't like we'd be chasing a killer unless something really big came up.

16

Mark went off to talk to Roy and the shifters who were searching. I checked with the rest of what I thought of as my team. Nothing new.

Ms. Flor was still enjoying herself exploring and said she'd be at Jan's tonight, but not to worry about her.

It left me with no choice but to head back to Mrs. V for magic studies. And I guess a recap of our conversation with Phillip. Something was up, but I had the distinct feeling it was more about me than the murder.

I stopped at Jan's and picked up coffees and pastries before heading off to Mrs. V.

My familiar had been suspiciously quiet, so I thought out at him. "Anything we can use to find the killer?"

"The shifters are searching the edges of the island. I do not think it is a useful way to find this killer, but they are unable to understand me. So, we animals continue to do valuable work."

"If you need to communicate to a shifter or a witch, tell me. I can text them."

He knew I could do this because we'd used the tactic on

the last case. I couldn't be sure he was manipulating us so the birds and animals would get the credit, but it would be just like him.

"The trail from the body to the front of the house is clear. The shifters know this, but perhaps they have not passed it along?"

Definitely some professional jealousy. What had I created?

"I'll let everyone know," I said. "Anything else?"

"I heard them say some vehicle brought the body. That must be one of the things you attach to the back of your bicycle, right?"

Since no cars or other powered vehicles were allowed on the island, the answer was yes. The various boats that traveled between Henbane and Sechelt were too small for someone to sneak a car over. And there were no gas stations, and too many people who would smell a combustion engine at work.

"Why can't anyone find the place he was murdered?" This was the problem we struggled with every time. Some spell confused the trail, or pepper covered the scent.

"The shifters think a spell. Not one to cover the scent, but one that stops it. The vermin agree. We are working what I think you call a search grid. We will find where the spell ends."

I thanked him and promised to fill the food stands I'd placed around the main path as payment for the searchers. The hunt was slowed by the fact that some of the animals were nocturnal and others were diurnal. And they needed to eat, feed their young, and all kinds of normal animal activities. Despite that, they'd come through on every case so far with a critical piece of information that led to solving the case.

Mrs. V's door was ajar and I stepped through carefully. It should be safe, but this might be a test.

"Come into the kitchen," she called. "We have things to talk about."

I poured the coffees into mugs and put the pastries on a plate. Mrs. V didn't drink out of cardboard cups or eat off a paper bag ripped open on the table.

"You don't need to bring me a bribe every day," she said as she reached for the chocolate croissant.

"Not a bribe," I said. "I needed something and it's rude not to share."

She nodded and pointed to the pendant. "It has a spell. Only specific people can open it. Have you tried?"

"Like the box the talismans came in?" Elias, my contractor, had found the box and told me it was locked. I'd opened it without much effort.

"Yes. Did you try?"

I thought back to when we found it under Martin's body. "No. We took photos and put it in the evidence bag."

She picked it up and pressed around the edge, where a normal one would have a clasp. "If I close my eyes, I can feel where it unlocks," she said. "It must be keyed to a specific person, or bloodline."

"Like DNA?" Did we have to pass it around the island looking for the right witch?

"From what I've researched, similar to DNA, but not exactly the same. And I can answer your next question. It's not likely to be to someone on this island since Mr. Light lived in the wider world."

"There will be other witches here in a few days," I said, "but I guess we can't really ask everyone to try."

"There is one more witch here from the mainland," she said.

"Who? Ms. Flor? I can ask her."

"I misspoke. There is a witch who lives here now but grew up elsewhere." She glared at me.

"Oh. Of course. Me." I reached for the pendant.

She pulled it away. "Not yet," she said. "You need to learn some protection spells first."

"But if it has a clue?"

"If it has a protection, we could lose you."

She didn't offer any other details around 'lose me'. It could mean more than just killing me. I could go into a coma, or have my powers burned out, or probably a hundred other things. I put my hands around my mug to stop me from reaching for the pendant.

"The talismans are the next problem," Mrs. V said. "They were in a box keyed to you. That means whoever locked them away intended for you to find them."

"Then I should be able to understand what they mean."

We were sure the objects were related to the person behind the killings. When Carly, the last killer to die trying to talk about the night my mother screwed up, told us about her mother, there were fifteen people on the list. There were fifteen talismans. If we could link them to either the victims or murderers, we should be able to trace the others. Prevent more deaths and stop the witch in control.

"It's not that simple. Like everything else, because you grew up as a non-magical human, there are gaps. Perhaps you should have knowledge of a spell to unlock their secrets, or you are too young, or your hidden power is needed. Patience. We will find the answers."

"Should I have a talisman?" I asked because maybe that was the missing item. A matching object that released whatever spell was disguising them.

"You can create one if you want, but not until you know

your power, and your magical education advances beyond what an eight-year-old can master. These are powerful tools, or they can be. And like most magic, they can be used against a witch. I will show you how to make your own when it's more appropriate."

Another thing to wait for. "Shall we start the lessons?" The sooner we began, the sooner I could head out and solve the murder.

17

There was nothing to follow up on by the time I headed home after lessons. D was still compiling the information he'd found on the names we had for the secret group Martin came to meet. Lilibeth and Doc Rene were still working through a series of tests to find out if a spell was used on him. Either to kill him, subdue him so he was easier to murder, or to hide the trace of his scent when moving him to Azalea's garden.

Mark sent a text to say it was nothing to worry about. Some things just took time and when we had some answers, we'd move fast.

As much as I didn't want to run into Phillip after the interview, I needed time to recharge. My guest, Zinnia Flor, had called to say she was going to take an early night so wouldn't be at Jan's. I had no idea if this was going to be the normal interaction. Other guests would be arriving soon, and if they all were as self-sufficient as Ms. Flor, my business wouldn't take up much of my time.

I entered the apartment from the side door, climbing the

stairs as quietly as possible. All the sneaking in was a waste. Phillip was in the kitchen making scrambled eggs.

"Hi," I said. "Let me know when you're done so I can make a sandwich, please."

"Would you like to share my eggs?" he asked. "It's not too late to throw in a couple more."

A big part of me wanted to say no. If he was going to confront me again about the case, I'd rather just take a sandwich to my room. But the eggs smelled so great.

"Yes, please. I'll make tea if you put the kettle on." There wasn't much room for two people to cook at the same time. The kitchen was large, but most of that was the social space.

"I'll do that too," he said, taking the pan off the heat. He cracked two eggs in a bowl, added salt, pepper, and thyme, and poured the ingredients into the pan. He lit the burner under the kettle and returned the eggs to the heat.

"Okay, I'll clean up," I said. "I can't just freeload on your hospitality."

"Delighted to let you do the dirty work," he said.

Now, I was totally confused. His mood was friendly, and it was like the meeting earlier hadn't happened. Before all the suspicion, he was generally coldish but friendly. I didn't know whether to worry about the change or not. His emotions were firmly behind a shield.

"I want to apologize for this afternoon," he said. "I let my grief over losing Martin as a friend overcome my trust in Mark to solve the case."

He poured water over a mixture of tea and herbs in the pot and put the eggs on two plates.

"I guess I understand," I said. I took cups, milk, and honey from the counter and added them to the table.

"I'm also a little surprised by my feeling of responsibility toward you, Cossi. To keep you safe."

"You don't need to worry about me," I said. "Mrs. Vestum is doing a great job of training me. To be honest, I'm a little afraid of her." Maybe that would soothe any feelings of betrayal he held against me because she was now my mentor.

"Aren't we all," he said with a laugh. "Eat your eggs before they get cold."

When the empty plates were in the sink and we were both sipping our tea, Phillip leaned back on his stool and looked at me.

I was about to ask if I had something on my face when he said, "I promised your parents that I would look after you."

He'd said something like that when I first arrived, maybe even when he responded to my call for help.

"Like a godfather?" Another hole in my education. I'd just assumed everyone on the island, everyone in the paranormal world, were atheists. Or on second thought, maybe pagans, if that wasn't some kind of insult.

"When I was last visiting," Phillip said. "I suppose it was your father who asked me to do it. Your mother died so young."

I put my mug down without taking a sip. He'd talked to my dad about me? Why would Dad write me a letter warning me to stay away from Henbane if Phillip was supposed to take care of me?

Yep, I was speechless. Not the kind where all you can do is babble about being speechless, but actually unable to talk. So many questions were running around my brain that I couldn't pick one.

"I thought you knew," he said. "I came regularly. At least once a month."

He watched me, and I almost felt him reading my mind.

He couldn't but that was what I labeled the creepy feeling of someone, or something, in my head.

"What's wrong?" Destroyer asked.

"Nothing," I thought back. "Just a shock about something."

"You woke me up for nothing? The witch needs to train you more." I heard grumbling in my head, but I ignored it.

I found my voice and took a sip of tea before I asked, "Why did you visit us?" I had a fuzzy memory of someone talking to my parents in the kitchen while I fell asleep on the couch.

"I am sorry to surprise you," Phillip said. "I suppose your parents wanted to keep you from finding out you were a witch. In the last few years, you were at school when I came. Thinking back, possibly the last time we actually talked was just after you started first grade. No wonder you don't remember."

He hadn't answered my question. Did I want to risk annoying him by asking again?

Yes.

"But why? They left Henbane under such awful circumstances."

He took my empty mug and put it in the sink with the rest of the dishes.

"A few years after the... incident, your mother reached out. They were homesick but knew better than to return. I suppose I felt they deserved some contact with their community. Losing touch with your friends is awful, Cossi. I hope you don't ever find out how hollow it makes you feel."

"Loss is hard no matter who it is," I said. Does he think becoming an orphan and giving up everything you know is easy?

"It is," he said. "I promise I will try to be helpful and not worry that Mark seems determined to keep me in the dark about the investigation."

He left after that. Probably nothing sinister, but I couldn't help feeling like he wanted to avoid more questions.

18

I fell asleep as soon as I got into bed. My plan of reading the assigned books, scanning paranormal social media for clues about the people on the list, or just practicing a few spells all went away.

In the morning, I made a mental note for my growing list of requirements when I moved out — an office, or at least a desk in my room. Working in bed was not productive when you craved sleep.

Mark summoned us all to his house. Not Mrs. V, because she'd been called in to help Doc Rene. Whatever the doctor had found on the body was beyond Lilibeth's knowledge.

"I have some information on the names," D said as he walked into the living room.

Mark had put out a pot of coffee and mugs, and a big jug of water. We all had filled glasses. I flashed back to study sessions in university. The table was low, but the seats were comfortable.

"I have a few tidbits from the autopsy," Lilibeth said. "Anything from the animal search?"

"Before I answer that, is it normal to have such a hard time identifying something like cause of death?"

"Usually, the witch dies of natural causes," Mark said.

"So, if we're having such trouble, does that mean the killer was prepared with all kinds of covering spells? That it was premeditated?"

"It's hard to imagine someone walking around with an arsenal of spells ready to cover up their activities," D said.

"Then we might get some clues from that," I said. "Pre-meditation might be the weak point."

"We'll keep it in mind," Mark said. "What about the animals?"

I'd asked Destroyer for an update before I came over. "A weak trail that keeps cutting out. Like the spell is interrupted. He'll keep his team searching."

"I don't like that," Lance said. "Dolph has a handful of shifters out working with Roy, but communication isn't easy. He doesn't talk wolf, and we don't talk dog."

You would think the difference would be something like an accent, or a dialect, but no. Distinct languages. I have no idea how Destroyer manages to learn so many.

"I am special," he said as if I'd asked. "Let me in."

Mark nodded when I asked if it was okay. "No flying around, no shedding, and no pooping."

"I am a civilized bird," Destroyer said when I passed the rules on.

"When you're sober," I reminded him of the time Mrs. V gave him a tea to get rid of the effect of the beer.

I opened the patio door, and he waddled in and hopped onto the table.

"I have something to talk about before the updates," Mark said. He put his phone on the table. "I have a problem. I thought I had it under control but, it's getting worse."

"Whatever you need," Lilibeth said. "You have to be honest with us, though. We can't help if you hold things back."

Mark rolled his shoulders and nodded. "Someone is trying to control the investigation. Not just this one, all of them up to now. I don't know who it is. D, I was hoping you could trace the calls."

"How are they controlling you?" I thought back to the calls he'd taken, and the ones he'd ignored. He was keeping a secret, but not what I thought.

"I'll give you the details if you think it's critical for finding whoever it is, but I would prefer to keep it private." He waited for us to challenge him.

I felt all of his emotions. That made me more confident in his words. Guilt, fear, anger, and shame were all flowing from him.

Lilibeth spoke first. "We all have things in our past we're embarrassed about." She patted his shoulder. "I think if you haven't been able to figure out who this is by the threat, then it's probably not important to fixing the problem."

"Is it just through the phone?" D asked, pulling a small black box from his backpack.

"Yes. Texts and calls." Mark's body relaxed, as if telling us was the hardest part. "No emails. Nothing on the system that can be copied. I tried screen shotting the texts, but it just showed up blurry."

D picked up Mark's phone and turned it on. "Unlock it, please."

Mark tapped a code and the screen came alive. D put the box on top of the phone and pressed a button. "I'm cloning. Next time this person contacts you, I'll get it too. Just do what you normally do."

"Lately that's been ignoring," Mark said. "They haven't

acted on the threat so maybe they have something to lose too?"

"Why are the texts blurry in a screen shot?" I asked. "Technology or spell?"

D looked up from the blinking green light on the box. "Both? Either? Maybe a camera issue with Mark's phone?"

The light stopped blinking. D pulled out a new phone from his backpack and repeated the steps.

"This is a burner," he said. "The sender won't know I'm getting a copy, so don't worry. And from now on, don't ignore the texts. You said they called, right? How often? And anything particular about the voice?"

"The calls are new," Mark said. "I guess because I started ignoring the texts. It was one of those computer voices."

Lance picked up Mark's phone and scanned the texts. "Looks like they just want information."

"Things we couldn't share," Mark said. "The council is off the suspect list because I kept Phillip up to date as my rep. And Mrs. V has always known what's going on."

"We'll find them and expose whoever is doing this," Lance said. "You'll face whatever comes out of the secret being exposed, but I think it's better if you're part of the solution."

"I'll do some tracing," D said, "when I get time between researching witches that seem very interested in keeping their lives secret."

19

"Updates," Mark said. "We need something to go on."

"I guess I can go first," Lilibeth said. "Doc Rene and Mrs. V are still trying to find the poison. They found remnants of a spell, but there wasn't enough left to guess what it was. Or identify who cast it."

"So, it was poisoning? To keep him from fighting back?" Lance asked.

"We won't know until they find it," Lilibeth said. "Identifying something like that is hard. It's easier if you know what you're looking for. They've gone through the most likely and are brainstorming and testing for obscure ones."

Much like a tox screen in the mundane world. "Would it help to have some kind of animal come — I guess with me or Destroyer — to sniff out the ingredients?"

"Roy," Mark said. "He's not having much luck with the shifters."

Being able to talk to both Destroyer and Roy was useful, but at a distance I could only understand my familiar. Information translated from dog to crow to me meant lots of opportunity for mistakes.

"Destroyer, how well do you speak Roy's language?" I asked. I'd prefer not to get stuck at the clinic while everyone else followed clues.

"Perfectly. I assume you are thinking I work with the dog and pass on what he has to say so you can send these texts? It might work," he said. "If not, I can call you wherever I need you to be."

I passed that on. "Tell Roy to meet you at the clinic, and I'll text Mrs. V so she knows you're coming."

I let Destroyer out. He could give me updates and news while they worked.

Mark asked Lance to go next.

"We aren't finding anything," he said. "Something is definitely wrong if we can't even get a sniff of a clue. I don't mean like last time, at those blank spaces. Every scent is normal. And it shouldn't be."

Destroyer had said the faint trails were breaking up. But I'd passed that on before Mark's admission and plea for help.

"An eraser spell?" I asked.

D looked up from his notes. "There are a few, but only one or two that would be this effective."

"And that breaking up of the trail you told us about," Mark said. "The spells are sprinkled across whatever is erased, so it takes a while to clear everything. Good idea. Tell the animals and shifters to try identifying normal scents that are a little more intense than usual."

I must have looked confused because Lilibeth said, "They use the normal environment to overwhelm the new scents. So different places along the path will have different components."

The mood in the room brightened with a wash of hope. I passed on the information to Destroyer, who grumbled about witches who kept secrets but agreed it was a good idea. Lance sent a text to Dolph.

"What if Martin was dead from the poison and the stabbing was a cover-up?" I hoped I was on a roll with fabulous ideas. "I mean, we just assumed he'd been stabbed somewhere else, right?"

Four sets of eyes turned to me. No one spoke. Was it such a stupid idea?

"It would explain a lot," Mark said, "and erasing a trail would be easier if there's no blood."

"Give me a minute," Lilibeth said, taking her phone to the kitchen.

"And all the searching for a violent murder site is useless," Mark said. "More than useless, it's wasting time and resources."

"If this is the same person behind everything, it would make sense for them to change methods." D said as he typed something in his database.

"Should I tell Dolph to call off the search?" Lance asked.

"Not yet," I said. "We don't know if this is correct. It's just a guess, right?"

Lilibeth came back into the room. "So, they already figured out Martin was dead when his body was stabbed."

"And they didn't think it was a good idea to pass it along?" Mark asked.

"It's a bit more complicated than that," she said. "Doc Rene thought I noticed when we were examining the body. Mrs. V thought we hadn't gotten around to telling her. My call was half Mrs. V berating me for something I didn't do, and half me trying to politely remind Doc Rene we needed to hear everything. I guess we don't need to say that assumptions make it very hard to solve cases, right?"

"Did you get any new information?" I asked. What else might Doc Rene have missed telling us?

"The blood on the body wasn't Martin Light's. It was animal blood. Probably from a side of beef. There were no post or perimortem bruises, so however the killer transported him, it wasn't rough."

"Or it was long enough after death that nothing would show," I said.

"Not enough time," Lilibeth said. "For that to be the truth, rigor would have to pass."

"Let's move onto the last bit of update," Mark said. "We need our full concentration to process this new development."

"Phillip is talking to me again," I said. His revelation about visiting us didn't need to be aired here. Nothing to do with the case. "It might be just the death of his friend, but he's really shaken up."

"We can start interviewing the members of the research group," D said. "Six of them are still alive. My dad, we'll have to reach out by phone. We've talked to Lawson. Jeffery Peak, but given his memory issues, that might not come to anything. Valerie Nightshade, Effie Walsh, Sexton Bold. Only seven in total, but we have no idea who they told."

Valerie had known my parents. Was that another mark against them? I hoped not; if Valerie was a killer, I couldn't trust my sense of people.

"Who's Sexton Bold?" I hadn't met even a small percentage of the residents, so maybe he was a good suspect and the people I knew were just innocent bystanders.

"A shifter," Lance said. "One of Dolph's advisers."

"Let's give Doc Rene and Mrs. V some time to finish

their work," Mark said. "I think we start the interviews. Then we can decide what to do about giving new instructions for the search."

I wasn't going to be the one to tell Dolph we'd wasted time when we called off the trackers. But I thought again, perhaps the new 'looking for normal smells that are too strong or weak' might turn up the place where the killer put Martin's body on the transport.

20

U ntil I knew whether Valerie was a real suspect, the betrayal I felt would only grow. It was no use to remind myself she was kind and that I couldn't imagine her killing anyone. I needed to talk to her first.

"Are we going together?" I asked. "Or splitting up?"

"I'm going back to the clinic," Lilibeth said. "I hate to say it, but I worry we'll get the same answer from Doc Rene or Mrs. V as before. Something they 'think' we know will change the entire case."

"Why don't Mark and I talk to Sexton?" Lance said. "He's more likely to open up to another shifter. He lives in the village, and Dolph is there if we need to tell him to call his hunters back."

My wish granted. "Mark can tell if Sexton is lying, and I can read Valerie's emotions. That makes a lot of sense."

"I'll come with you," D said. "I don't think we should split up too much. I'm worried something else will fall through the cracks if we keep having to update each other rather than discuss what we all know."

"Meet tonight? Dinner at The Inner Spell. I can get Jan

to put together some take-out, and we have the big meeting room all ready to go. Only one of the chalets is booked, so it will be private."

And I can think about how to move into the main building while we're there.

"Lance and I'll get something from The Howling Place instead," Mark said. "It's on the way, and we can test if catering works for you, right? The logistics, I mean."

Jan had offered to take it on in partnership with Zoe from Food For Us. Adding Sheena into the mix would be a good move. I made a mental note to check in with Jan before my next set of guests arrived so he wasn't taken by surprise.

The ride to the earth witch village was only about fifteen minutes. The more I rode around the island, the fitter I became and the faster the trips were. When I first arrived, the same trip was about a half hour, and for the first few days, I was pretty sore afterwards.

Valerie's house was one of the first after the trees that marked the entrance. Two large redwoods that leaned toward each other like an arch. The earth witches were capable of using magic to do things nature couldn't.

"Come in," Valerie said as we walked toward the door. She, like a lot of the witches who lived here, knew when someone was approaching. Not just witches. I had a memory flash of Dolph opening his door as I stood staring at his house.

We followed her into the kitchen, the center of most houses here. Cookies cooled on the rack, and a cozy covered teapot waited for us.

"Have you come to talk about your mother and father?" she asked me. "D, your parents really need to return to Henbane soon."

"I'll pass that on," D said. "Maybe coming from you it will have a better result. Shall I pour?"

We settled in with teas that smelled like fresh lemons and ginger to go with the chocolate chip cookies.

"We need to talk about Martin Light," D said. "He was in the same group as you and a few others. Did you see him on the island?"

"Martin, no," she said, fussing over the arrangement of plates and cups. "We should have. I'm sure if you know about our mission, then you also know that we planned to have an in-person meeting at the festival."

"Did you talk to him online? Or on the phone?" I asked. The kitchen was as cozy as I remember from my last few visits. A comfortable collection of mismatched tableware on open shelves, candles and jars of herbs and powders on the back of the counter. Warm from the wood fired range.

"What do you actually know about our mission?" Valerie asked. "Before I talk about it, I need to know I'm not spilling any secrets. Cossi, I'm sure you can imagine the reaction if someone gets only half the story."

"We've already decided it's not a good idea to feed the rumor mill," D said. "Mrs. V told us you were looking for ways to help the mainland communities better fit into the non-magical world. They're finding it increasingly difficult to stay hidden without actually hiding."

"Not like what my mother did," I said. "The island isn't part of your mandate, right?"

She relaxed. I guess she'd been trying to walk a fine line between helping us solve the case and keeping the news about their group from getting out. That's what I read from the confusion of emotions spilling from her, anyway.

"Yes. The whole trend of non-magicals living their lives on social media is causing problems. Among other things, they tend to ignore anything or anyone around them when taking selfies or making their little videos. Nothing has actually happened, but we don't want to wait for a disaster before we look for a solution."

"What happens to the photo or video if it catches a paranormal or magical building?" I might be able to help if I knew more details. For the first time, my early life as a normal human might be an asset.

"Blurring," D said. "We developed that a long time ago. But now that everyone is taking random pictures, there is a huge risk someone will see a pattern and investigate."

"Exactly," Valerie said. "It's not just the people taking the videos and photos, it's people pulling together collections, and some kind of program that might actually notice first."

"AI," D said.

"Is the magic doing the blurring, or is the spell to blur it?" I couldn't think of a clearer way to put it.

"Both," Valerie said. "If a spell is in place for long enough, a magical field forms. It will dissipate if spells are removed, but we can't let people know what the business are called, or that earth witch gardens produce out-of-season food."

"I'll talk to Mrs. V about consulting with you," I said. "I have a few ideas, and it might just be as simple as creating a clearer and more current disguise spell. But that's not what we're here for."

"I don't think I can help with the case, Cossi. I did speak to Martin on the phone, but only to set up the coming meeting. We really haven't done anything more than form yet."

"If you think of something, will you let us know?" I asked.

"Of course. We owe you for sending that snake along to

our gardens. He brought his family, and we are no longer in a battle with slugs."

Clarence gave us a tip in the second murder, and payment came in the form of an 'all the slugs you can eat' buffet.

Something had been tugging at my attention during the discussion, and I finally identified it. Along the top of the wall was a thin rail holding decorative plates and small pieces of art. Almost every one of them had a tiny green turtle somewhere in the design.

"Is that turtle your emblem?" I asked. "It's cute."

Valerie was in the process of standing when I asked, and she sank back into her seat. Her face flushed and then went pale.

"Are you all right?" D asked. He reached for her wrist and put the back of his hand on her forehead.

"I'm fine. At my age, you expect to have a few funny turns. Don't fuss, Didier. You have a murder to solve."

I sent a text to Doc Rene as soon as we stepped outside her door. Valerie might be reluctant to have a doctor check her out, but I didn't want to risk losing someone who'd been so kind to me.

21

W e split up after that and I went back to Mrs. V's to look at the talismans again. She was still at the clinic, but I knew the code to cancel the spell on her security room — legitimately, I didn't hack her.

I brought out the bag and found her copy of The Compendium of Spells. I had a couple of hours before we were meeting at The Inner Spell to share our findings. Plenty of time to see if knowing that the turtle meant it related to Valerie had weakened whatever spell kept confusing us.

And time to work on my assigned reading.

The turtle was kind of the same as the ones on Valerie's art. More of a skeleton sketch. Like artists did to get the placing and shapes right, but definitely the same. The shape of the stone was sort of round, sort of squared off, with a dip in the center. That's where the turtle drawing was scratched. With my minimal training, I knew to set a ward around me to keep any explosions or turning to toads confined. Then I'd have to look through the book and try to figure out what kind of spell to do.

Yes, I could have waited for Mrs. V, but a tiny part of me wanted to show her I knew what I was doing when I removed the spell. Another part of me was nervous that I'd completely screw it up and end up in the middle of a magical blast zone.

That part was bigger, but I chose to ignore it.

I put the remaining stones back in the bag and into the secured room. Next, I put the turtle stone and book on the table. The wards were fairly simple spells so I placed them to protect the entire kitchen.

I opened the book and ran my finger down the index in the back.

An hour later, I'd run through all of the summoning spells I could cast — thinking I could call the stone out of the magic that kept confusing our view. Nothing worked, and I was starving from all the energy it took.

I made tea and found a box of crackers. The next set of spells to try were cleansing and clarity. Even if I had the time before meeting my friends, I was wrung out, so more than likely I would do something wrong. I took my notebook and made a list of the new spells I'd learned in the process and a note where to start next. Mrs. V would be proud of how successful I'd been. With the casting, not the results. None of them gave me what I needed, but a witch knows when a spell goes right.

I decided to head up to The Inner Spell early. Get the room ready. Check on Ms. Flor, if she was there. And take one last look at the accommodation for my incoming guests.

WHEN I GOT THERE, I started with the chalets. All were fully ready, and the freshness spell I'd cast worked perfectly. All I needed to do was add the welcome baskets on the morning of arrival.

Ms. Flor was home, and she thanked me for checking in. She was resting up for another fun evening and would take care of herself.

In the main building, the rooms were ready, the kitchen was stocked with coffee and tea. The rest would come later in the week.

The last thing I did was go through the rooms to see if one was a good choice for my own home in the future. None were. A problem for after the festival. I'd had no choice of a home when I first arrived. Phillip was my mentor, and he had room for me. Mrs. V took over the training, but her house was too small for a permanent guest.

I put out everything we'd need for dinner and arranged chairs at the end of a refectory table to make it cozier. I'd chosen it so my guests could sit in small groups at the same table if they wanted to chat or conduct group sessions.

Mark walked in with Roy beside him. "Everyone is on their way," he said. "I thought it might be a good idea for you to translate any decisions to Roy. He's been focused on finding the trail that we realized doesn't exist."

"You could have told me earlier," Roy said.

"How?" I asked. "We can't communicate over longer distances."

"That crow would find a way to tell me," Roy said.

"And you shouldn't keep secrets from me," Destroyer added. "Do you want me constantly sitting on your shoulder?"

I rolled my eyes and told Mark the conversation he only heard as soft barks from Roy.

"I thought your familiar could read your mind," he said.

"I was busy trying to solve the puzzle," Destroyer said. "I

will listen now to make sure I am not wasting everyone's time."

"It's only been a few hours," I said. "And we didn't know if we were right."

"Excuses." The word came from Destroyer, with Roy a split second later.

"We'll update all of you, and Dolph," I said. "We should know if Doc Rene and Mrs. V learned anything when Lilibeth gets here."

D joined us, effectively ending the conversation between me and the animals that only I could understand.

"Lance and Lilibeth are a few minutes behind," he said. "Mark, did you get any calls from your... let's call them your friend?"

"Not my friend," Mark said. "I guess it will do. I got a text and six missed calls."

"That tracks with what I received on the clone. So, we know that part works."

His disappointment shone out of him as a greenish yellow. This seeing emotions as colors thing could be nauseating.

"Did you find anything?" I had to ask because knowing what he was feeling didn't guarantee it was about finding the witch trying to control Mark.

"It's going to take a while. The calls are routing around the world and not long enough for me to get close. You might need to talk to this person. Keep them on long enough to trace."

"If I put them on speaker, won't they know?" Mark asked. "Will the clone do that feedback thing?"

"Not speaker," D said. "If they call, I guess I mean when, not if, you take it and go outside to talk. I'll start tracing them."

"If the voice is distorted, we won't learn anything from hearing them." I wondered if recording the call was an option.

"We don't know what kind of magic they are using," D said. "Just do what you normally do."

"If it happens when you aren't around?" Mark asked. His emotion was a trembling white shade.

"The clone will ring," D said.

Lance and Lilibeth arrived with dinner. We settled in for the meal and the beer he'd brought in a small keg. Food before updates sounded great to me. Those crackers hadn't made a dent in the gnawing hunger from casting spells.

22

I t didn't take long to eat the food Sheena sent with Lance and Lilibeth. Warm, fresh sourdough bread, cold cuts, salad, and for dessert, puff pastry filled with custard and raspberries. Roy wolfed down a few slices of roast beef.

"Okay," Mark said. "We need a quick update and to find some new actions." He'd taken on the role of leader. It made sense because he was a cop, and since there was not much progress, we needed all the professional viewpoints we could get.

"Destroyer is listening," I said. "He knows we think there's no murder site with blood."

"I'll go first," Lilibeth said. "It's definitely murder by poison. The animals might find the scent of it being made. He ingested a poison that caused his heart to burst. Lily of the Valley leaves in his digestive system was the last piece of the puzzle."

"It wouldn't have taken long," D said. He was hunched over his laptop. "It says here that the poison will mimic a heart attack and, unless treated immediately, is fatal."

"So, we send the searchers looking for Lily of the Valley?" I asked. "Don't the earth witches have it in their poison garden?"

"The killer probably thought that through," Lilibeth said. "Scents will lead to the garden because they are strongest there."

"Not necessarily," Lance said. "Were the leaves cooked? I mean, it's unlikely he ate them voluntarily, right?"

"Ground up, but not very finely," Lilibeth said.

"We can search for that," Destroyer said.

"It will make a difference to the scent," Lance said before I passed on Destroyer's comment.

"He's right," Roy barked at me.

I wanted to cover my ears, but two of the voices were in my head.

"Is there a risk to anyone following the scent?" I remembered my mother warning me when I tried to pick the pretty little white bells of the flowers in our garden. Everything about the plant was poison except its perfume.

"It will be fine," Lance said, "as long as no one tastes the traces they find. We have no idea if the killer set a preservation spell to keep the poison effective."

I passed on the information to Destroyer.

"I will order the army to take care. This is likely to be the job of my ground troops."

I found myself asking the same question all the time these days: what have I created?

"I'm off," Roy said and walked to the door. He stared at me until I went to open it.

"I'll text Dolph," Lance said. "It feels like we've actually made progress."

The room was filled with a rosy, emotional uplift that only I could see.

"Anything else?" D asked.

"They don't think you'll get any more information from the body," Lilibeth said. "He doesn't seem to have any relatives or close friends on the mainland, so Mrs. V thought we should have his funeral here. They will keep the body fresh until the case is closed."

"Sexton didn't know much about Martin," Mark said. "Dolph called him in when we asked him to, and he sat in on the interview."

"It meant Sexton couldn't lie or refuse to answer," Lance reminded us. "He had nothing to do with the murder but was expecting Martin to visit him that day."

D updated the notes and then looked at me.

"Nothing more about the killing," I said, thinking over the discussion we had with Valerie. Was it a good idea to add what I'd noticed about the turtle? "The committee was looking into helping the paranormals who live in the non-magical communities to avoid being exposed now that everyone is taking photos everywhere."

D explained the fear that some person, or AI, would recognize a pattern of blurred photos at locations and make a link. "If anyone starts investigating, the truth is likely to come out."

"What do paranormals in smaller communities do?" I asked.

"They don't," Mark said. "A few solitaries live in the outskirts of small towns, but they're written off as oddballs, mostly. If they feel like they're being looked at too closely, they move. Big cities are the safest places to hide ourselves."

"So, she knew Martin online," D said. "Valerie wasn't concerned she hadn't seen him on Henbane. The group was going to get together at the festival."

"They'll still do that," Lance said. "There will be plenty of mainlanders to replace Martin."

"True, he was the only one who lived off-island," D said. "They'll need someone to represent the real problem."

"Maybe my guest, Ms. Zinnia Flor, will step in," I said. "I'll suggest it to Mrs. V. That way, they can get started before the rest of festival guests arrive. Until we know otherwise, it's possible the committee is the reason he was killed."

"The list is in the database," D said. "We can check up on them all, but why would a member be killing off the participants?"

"Slowing down the work," Mark said. "Sabotage from the inside, right?"

"So, we have one more clue," D said. "Are we clearing Sexton and Valerie? It is progress to narrow the suspects."

"Dolph's presence means Sexton couldn't lie, but he didn't have to volunteer something we didn't ask." Lance looked at Mark. "Can you think of any loophole we left?"

"We asked him if he killed Martin Light," Mark said. "He denied it. Unless he didn't know the victim's name, there's no way he could have lied. And he was part of the group, so not likely."

"Did you ask if he knew who did?" I asked.

"Yes," Lance said. "He didn't, but he was certain it couldn't be part of the committee because they were all vetted. Every one of them saw the danger."

"Why are most of the committee members from Henbane?" I asked.

"He said it was our ability to keep the island invisible," Lance said. "We have the experts; the mainland has the problem."

"All over the world?" I asked. The most likely suspects

would be people who were against the aims of the group. But no one would be willing to expose themselves to normal humans. Too big a risk.

"Yes," Mark said. "Sexton was pretty open about the aims of the committee. In varying degrees, the problem is growing. Tourist sites are a weak link. We stay away from proximity to them, but these days, visitors are treating entire cities like they're rides at Disneyland, taking pictures of houses and businesses as if they are some reconstructions of ancient monuments."

"What about Valerie?" Lilibeth asked. "Did she have any secrets?"

I looked at D to see if he was holding back suspicions. He shook his head.

"I can't believe she would do anything like that," I said. "She told us details about the committee and the problem the other communities face."

"And?" Mark asked. "You're holding something back."

I didn't want to muddy the investigation, but maybe it was all connected.

"I noticed all the symbols of turtles in her house. It matched one of the talismans. Not completely, but it's definitely related."

"And she didn't answer," D said. "Remember, she got dizzy and pale? We didn't want to push."

"Note it in the database," Mark said. "We need to follow up with the other people on the list before going back to her. See if you notice any other matching symbols. But focus on the murder."

23

No miraculous clue from Destroyer, no mice or squirrels running to tell me they'd found the place or method of Martin's poisoning. It was late. I headed back to Phillip's to hide in my room and study. Murder or not, Mrs. V expected me to continue my training.

Before we split up, we agreed to interview other committee members the next day. I still didn't think any of them were killers, but maybe they'd have a suggestion for other names to add to our list.

IN THE MORNING, Phillip was in the kitchen when I woke, so we shared toast and tea. This time he watched as I made the tea mixture and set it to brew. I know it's silly, but his trust in me started my day on a high.

"Can you give me any news?" he asked. "I don't want to interfere, but I feel like I can help if you let me."

His frustration threaded through his emotions. I sympathized, but there wasn't much I could share.

"It's better to keep the investigation under wraps," I said.

"I can say we don't have a real suspect yet, but we're making headway."

"What do you have, Cossi? I don't want to have to call the council together in order to get an update from Mark, but we won't just sit by while he takes his time. The festival is in danger; the island's reputation as a safe place is under threat."

Normally Mark would update Phillip as his council representative, but this time the victim was a friend. It made sense to keep everything under wraps.

"Mrs. Vestum is working with us," I said. "I'm sure she can keep the council updated."

"Taking my place in that, too?"

His emotions spilled out of his control. Anger spiked, and fear. I wasn't sure if the fear was about the murders or his role. He'd never struck me as someone who needed validation that way. I felt sorry for him. Maybe if I gave him something that wasn't part of the investigation, it would help him leave us to the job.

"There is one thing," I said. "What do you know about talismans?"

"As a way to identify a killer?" He sipped his tea. "Do you have one?"

"Mrs. V said I shouldn't try yet for me, but I did notice something." I wasn't going to tell him about the ones Mrs. V was protecting. Until we knew who they belonged to, I couldn't trust anyone. "Valerie Nightshade has turtles on all her decorations. When I asked her about it, she got ill."

"Is she with Doc Rene?" he asked. "A witch of her age is vulnerable to even the mildest infection."

"She said she was fine. But I wonder if that's her talisman. Do you know?"

He got the teapot and refilled our cups. My tactic

worked. The emotional storm from before was calmed. A distraction was all he needed.

"Most of us made them years ago," he said. "I haven't seen one for a while. I guess it was just a fad. For years we wore them on bracelets or necklaces. They reinforce power, like a little battery boost. I lost mine when I went swimming shortly after we created them."

A battery? I guess that could be what Mrs. V meant when she said they were powerful tools.

How much more could I ask before I gave away the secret about having fifteen of them? Oh yeah, and not being able to reliably describe them because of some unknown spell? I was almost there, but if he knew who had them, it would save us a lot of time.

"Is it the same as the emblem? Like the beech leaf we found when we were searching for Jeffery Peak?"

"No. It could be a completely different symbol. For instance, my emblem is a stalk of papyrus. Representing my leaning toward books and scrolls. If I remember correctly, my talisman was marked with a cat's paw."

"How long ago did you make them?"

"I was probably around fourteen or so. That makes it almost a hundred years."

"No wonder you can't remember it," I said. "Should I get an emblem?"

"At some point. You will know your... I guess 'calling' is the best expression. Then you'll choose an emblem. It's nothing to do with power, Cossi. More like a logo."

"Do you remember who was in the group? The ones who made the emblems."

He shifted in his seat like I'd asked a difficult question. Maybe a hundred years was enough for him to forget the entire group, but surely he would remember one or two names.

"We wouldn't be the only ones with talismans," he said. "Valerie's would be hundreds of years old. But there were a few I remember. D's father had one but lost it a few years ago. It's possible that Leanne Macy was one of us too, but you can't ask her."

No, she was the first witch murdered.

"Okay, that helps. Anyway," I said, "are you going to ask Mrs. V for an update on the case?" I really didn't want him to know anything about our investigation. I didn't have a solid reason, but his mood swings were hard to manage. So, I hoped he'd say she was capable of handling this case.

He frowned at me and didn't answer right away. He lifted the lid of the teapot and swirled the leaves in the last of the water. Taking a sniff of the contents, he grimaced.

"Bitter," he said. "I think I should trust you and your team. If Mrs. Vestum thinks it's best to keep secrets, then I must trust her. She is the protector, after all."

24

I got a text telling me to go to Mrs. V's house for the update. Since we hadn't had a chance to interview the people we'd planned, it must have meant there was a development overnight.

I met D on the way, and we picked up coffee and treats at Jan's to take with us.

"We may have found a trail," Destroyer said in my mind.

I stopped walking to talk to him.

"What do you mean?" This case was full of maybes.

"In the reports from the rodent unit of my army, I detected a pattern. This evening, we will attempt to follow it."

"Can't you do it now?" I was convinced that finding where he was killed would lead us directly to the murderer.

"Rodents are sleeping. I need many of them to line the places where the scent is. Tell the witches and shifters we will be out and not to disturb us. Rodents are easily distracted."

I passed it on to D. "I guess seeing them lined up might show the gaps in the trail that they can close."

"Fill the feed stations today," Destroyer ordered me. "The unit will be hungry, and their food gathering time will be taken up with their searching duties."

I agreed to stop by and fill what I thought of as food ATMs. Easier to manage than having a backpack full of seeds and nuts. What surprised me the most was none of the animals took more than a fair share. A squirrel told me they missed the scavenging stories they shared, but easy food was better.

"So, at some point tonight, mice, squirrels, chipmunks, and voles, and all kinds of other animals are going to line up so we can see the path they keep losing?" D asked.

"Correct," Destroyer said.

"Then we should be there," I said. "Where do we meet you?"

"I will inform you when we are close," Destroyer said.

I thanked him and started toward Mrs. V's home again.

INSIDE, we passed on the information and all agreed to be ready to ride to wherever Destroyer said.

"It's likely to be over by the solitaries," Lance said as he texted Dolph. "Maybe we should head there at dusk."

Mrs. V told D to alert the witches.

"I admit I am very excited," she said. "This is possibly the first time animals and humans have worked together so well. This can only be good for Henbane."

For once I felt like I'd done the right thing. I had so much to learn about life as a witch that I always expected to be corrected, or see disappointment flow out of the people around me.

"I also have some information about the talismans," I said. "Anything from Doc Rene?"

Lilibeth shook her head. "There won't be any more information. I'm just glad the poison is going to lead us to where he was killed."

"What about the talismans?" Mrs. V asked. "We can't waste time here. You have committee members to interview, and this evening might end in an arrest."

I told them what Phillip explained. "So, someone knows what these are. He told me your dad lost his, D."

"None of those are lost," D said. "You have them."

"I remember a little about this," Mrs. V said. "Most of the teenagers on the island made their own talismans. I haven't seen a single one lately."

"How many teenagers?" I asked. On the mainland that could be hundreds or thousands if a fad caught on.

"Thirty or so," Mrs. V said. "I suppose most of them might be tucked away like jewelry. But someone seems to have collected half of them."

"Do you remember what the symbols are?" I asked.

"Only a few. And none of the ones we have match my memory." She pulled a sheet of paper toward her. "Let me work on it. But I think Batiste's was an albatross. There is nothing in the ones you have that looks like one of those."

There was.

I had the advantage of knowing how different the turtle was to the actual image. I didn't trust my photos, so I went and pulled out the talisman I thought belonged to D's dad.

"This one," I said, putting it on the table. "Look, it's rudimentary, but that squared off C could be a wingspan."

"What are you talking about?" Lance asked. "The image is a rune of protection."

Before everyone could chime in with what they saw, I held up my hand. "We all see different things, right? I think I see the real image. And it's under layers of spells. I saw the relationship between the turtle in Valerie's home and the talisman, after all."

"And they were collected for you," Mark said. "That's why Elias thought the box was locked and you were able to open it."

That was something I hadn't thought through. Yes, Elias said they were on my land so they belonged to me. But how would anyone know I was going to return to Henbane, let alone lease that piece of land for my business?

"Unless we think Batiste is involved with the murder, this isn't getting us closer to an arrest," Mark said. "We should interview the committee members now."

"My dad wouldn't be involved in something like this," D said. "And he's been off island for a couple of years now."

And Phillip said Batiste had lost his. Perhaps if the one with the albatross did turn out to be his, then it was stolen rather than lost. But Mark had a point; it wasn't a clear connection to the murder.

"About time he came home," Mrs. V said. "That's for another time. I've contacted all the committee members to let them know the interviews are approved. And we will need a new off-island representative. I will give you the name when we decide."

They'd have plenty of choices in a few days. All of my guests were candidates, and others who were staying with friends and relatives.

We split the names. Lawson, Sexton, and Valerie were crossed off. D said he'd call his dad to talk, leaving Jeffery Peak, Effie Walsh, our grocer, and whoever was added.

Lilibeth and Lance went off to talk to Effie. Mark and I would see what Jeffery might remember from his past since the spell damaged his more recent memories.

25

Jeffery was holed up in his cabin. He was a solitary witch and would go for days without seeing any other person. He was also a member of the council and didn't just follow the majority of the members in a vote — I'd gotten approval of my business thanks to him.

When his friend was murdered, he'd been kidnapped and moved around the island to keep him from being rescued. One of the spells the killer cast on him stripped his memory of the event. And more than that, it also took his memory of an experiment he'd been conducting with the help of the victim.

I hadn't seen him for a couple of weeks, so I had no idea if he'd recovered any of the missing memories. Or if they were gone for good. Mrs. V put him on this committee, so he must have been capable enough to solve a huge problem.

"You can go ahead and lead the questioning," Mark said as we parked our bikes against a huge tree at the entrance to Jeffery's home. "He likes you, so it might make him more comfortable."

I was okay with that plan. I might not be an official cop, but sitting and taking notes was boring.

"Door's unlocked," Jeffery called as we set foot on the veranda. "Come on in."

The last time I'd been inside his home, it was a mess. The murderer had broken in and tossed everything around. We'd assumed he was searching for the notes on this grand experiment, but we never got proof. We knew for sure the murderer did the damage because my animals knew. And it was the first time I met Destroyer.

Now it was tidy. The papers and books were on the large table in stacks. All the herbs and contents of his kitchen cupboard had been cleaned up. A fire burned in the hearth, and the aroma of freshly baked bread flowed from the kitchen.

Jeffery stepped through the doorway, a plate of muffins in his hand. He'd gained back the weight he'd lost as a captive, and regained his retired biker look: a Harley t-shirt and black jeans with black socks. His leather jacket and biker boots were near the door on a coat rack and mat, respectively.

"Tea is brewing," he said. "Are you hungry?"

The muffins were steaming on the plate, blueberry and chocolate chips. Even if I wasn't starving again, I'd find room.

Mark helped him set up the table, leaving me to bring the tea and mugs. If we weren't here to interview him about a murder, it would be a lovely visit.

When we were settled, Jeffery said, "The latest murder. That's why you want to talk, right?"

"Saying it like that feels like we aren't done with these events," I said. "Let's hope that's not the case. Yes, we're trying to find some clues."

"Let me start by telling you I didn't do it. I don't have any odd blank spaces in my memory, either. This time I have no involvement — I think."

"Good to hear," I said. "What do you know about the victim?"

"Not a lot. He reached out to Mrs. V with the problem," he said. "We agreed to come up with a few solutions. Perhaps test some out."

I made a mental note to ask for Mrs. V's notes on the committee. "Do you know of anyone who might kill to stop you succeeding?"

Jeffery took a moment to think. I took that as a positive. If he didn't have a suspicion, he'd have said so right away.

Mark's phone buzzed. He looked at the screen, up at me, then ignored the call.

"I don't like to think anyone would kill someone," Jeffery said. "But recent events have proved any number of people will kill for reasons no one can understand. No name comes to mind. Why would someone want our world exposed?"

"It might not be that," Mark said. "We can't assume the motive is stopping the committee. It horrifies me to admit it, but someone might not care about the wider consequences."

His phone buzzed again. He looked down at the text and then responded with a thumb's up emoji.

"There is something," Jeffery said. "I cannot rely so much on my memory. I have retrieved tiny flashes that make no sense. I hope this will continue and eventually I will connect the shards into a coherent whole. But I am experiencing deja vu with some of the details. Pieces of information that don't feel new to me. Perhaps it's time to ask for help with these seeking rituals I've been doing alone."

"What details?" I asked.

"Some of the examples the off-island communities are concerned with," he said. "I can try to list them for you. The ones that are more concerning are where I feel I know a solution."

"As if you've solved this problem before?" Mark asked. "Recently? Perhaps this is your experiment?"

"Recently and in my past. I cannot be sure, but I think it was with your mother's work, Cossi."

I'd been told she was trying to reinforce the protective spell on the island when she exposed it for a few seconds. And that it hadn't been necessary because the spell was strong. Now we have another indication that perhaps the island had been in danger.

"Were you involved that night?" Mark asked. His emotions radiated protection over me. Taking on the questioning so I didn't have to dig into the reasons we fled.

"It is possible," Jeffery said. "If someone who was with your parents said I was there too, I'm in no position to deny it now that my memories are untrustworthy."

"Something for us to talk about when this case is solved," I said.

We were getting distracted again. Suspecting these killings had something to do with my parents wasn't proof and wouldn't solve this case.

"I look forward to that," he said. "Talking with someone who knows so little about us is stimulating."

"We should find out what Effie has to say," Mark said. "And it's only a few hours before we'll have a trail to follow."

We said our goodbyes and I promised to visit Jeffery after the rush of the festival.

"What was that call?" I asked. "You almost asked my advice, right?"

"The person who's trying to control me," Mark said. He

rubbed his temples. "Then it was D. He told me to answer it next time because that's the only way he can trace the call."

"Are you okay?" I asked.

"Headache. This case is causing them. I'm tired of running around in circles. We need to get this all settled before the festival."

26

"What now?" I asked. "Should we try to meet Lance and Lilibeth? See if Effie had an idea that will help?"

"Maybe," Mark said. "D might have talked to his dad already, too. Did you think it was weird for Mrs. V to say he should come home?"

How would I know what was weird?

"Is it part of her job? Making sure people don't lose touch with Henbane?"

"Her job is what she decides it is," he said. "I guess if a witch is away for too long it might have an effect, but people have stayed away a lot longer than the Rothtects, and nothing has gone wrong."

"But now people are being murdered," I said. "That's a big change. Who else is away?"

He rubbed his head for a moment. I thought he was trying to recall a list, but his wince betrayed the fact his headache hadn't disappeared.

"I don't require people to register," he said. "Probably

twenty or so witches, and Dolph could tell us which shifters left."

"Long term?" I asked. The population of the island couldn't be more than a couple of hundred people all told. Unless there was another hidden village.

"Someone is always going between Sechelt and Henbane, especially now with the festival. I meant about twenty witches who've been away longer than you've been here. So, a month or more."

"What happens with their homes? Do they use a spell to keep them from filling up with mice and spiders? Or does someone check on them?"

"Both. D's parents have a farm, Lance looks after it while they are away. Is this going somewhere?"

"There you are." Phillip walked toward us.

We'd made it to the bike parking lot while we talked. So, it wasn't like he'd been searching the island. His expression was tight, and I couldn't see any of his emotions. One of the benefits of this new color thing was no snooping required. I could apply my power and get past the superficial, but I'd decided that was a boundary I wouldn't cross without reason.

"Do you need something?" Mark asked.

"I don't. I have some information for you," Phillip said. "You've been investigating people you know are here, but I thought I would help by finding out who has returned home or shown up early for the festival."

I knew he couldn't read my mind, but that's exactly what I was getting at in our conversation.

"Good timing," Mark said. "We were just talking about that."

"I suppose I would have thought of it earlier if I was still the representative." He waved away my reminder that he was too close to the victim. "Yes, I understand the reasons. I have a list. People who were here at the time of Martin's death."

He handed Mark a sheet ripped from a notebook. I couldn't read it, but there were six names listed, with a comment on each.

Mark took a photo and sent it out to the team as a heads up. "I'll add it to our database." I checked and saw his text said we should talk soon and to come to Jan's.

"Glad I could help," Phillip said. "I suppose you've made progress?"

He had no intention of letting us just do our work. The main emotion he let slip through his guard was frustration, not curiosity.

"I'll speak to Mrs. V about what we should share," Mark said. "You know from past cases giving out information too early makes things much harder."

"But if we send out a general call for tips, we... I mean you, might get the lead you're missing."

"And we'll get a lot of nosy witches taking up our time," Mark said. "You will know as soon as we make an arrest."

I stayed out of the conversation. I'd given Phillip more than enough reasons to be irritated with me. Leaving him for Mrs. V being the biggest reason, but I didn't want him to tell me to get out immediately when I told him I was planning to move into The Inner Spell.

"And perhaps I can advise on how best to prevent future problems," Phillip said. "We would hate to have a murder in the middle of the festival, right?"

"It's not up to me," Mark said. "If it was, no one would have been murdered."

Phillip pursed his lips, but his guard snapped into place before I could sense if it was anger at Mark or at himself.

"I'll let you get on with it," he said. "I've done what I can to help. I won't interfere unless you ask me for assistance."

He walked away.

"It is helpful," I said. "The list."

"Yes, and too convenient that we'd just finished talking about it when he handed it over."

"You think he's listening in on our conversations?"

Mark closed his eyes and reached to test the air as if we were in a large bubble. When he was done, he looked in his pockets and asked me to check mine.

"Nothing," he said as he touched the articles. "We'll check our backpacks in Jan's. I think it was just a coincidence. I mean, we'd run out of residents to talk to, right?"

I didn't say anything because coincidences happen. And there were lots of reasons Phillip would come to the same conclusion as I did at the same time. Now that I knew there were surveillance spells, I'd be more careful. I'd also look at the index in my copy of The Compendium of Spells because there were types I hadn't noticed.

We both received texts confirming everyone was on the way. Time to plan what to do with Phillip's list.

27

W e settled in Jan's at a large table near the kitchen. Beer, tea, and water all round. It was too early for dinner and too late for lunch, and frankly, I'd been snacking all day so I didn't need anything.

"Effie was annoyed at us," Lance said. "Not unusual for her. She'd met Martin when he arrived. He came into the store to buy a few items. He told her he was particular about his food and would likely be making all his meals."

"So how did someone poison him?" I asked.

"He could have drunk it," Lilibeth said. "A strong tea or a dark beer. Something with enough flavor to cover the taste of the plant."

"Beer is more likely," Mrs. V said. "Cooking a poisonous plant can reduce the potency. There was nothing in his stomach to help us pinpoint what the killer used to carry the poison. The leaves we found in his stomach could have been floating in anything."

That was odd, although I guess she didn't say there was

nothing in his stomach, just that they couldn't tell which was poisoned. "Is Effie a suspect?"

"She's been traveling back and forth to Sechelt to fill orders for foodstuff we don't produce. Specific tea blends, breakfast cereal, sodas," Lilibeth said. "I can't see how she'd have time."

So, we were out of people to interview unless the ones on Phillip's list could help.

"I invited your guest to join the committee," Mrs. V said.

"Zinnia Flor?"

My suggestion worked. Mrs. V thought bringing her in was a good idea. I'd take my wins where I found them.

"The problem hasn't gone away," Mrs. V said. "She has lived in a few different communities and is a historian. Unless you've changed your mind about her and think she killed Martin Light to take his place, she is acceptable."

"She's been socializing all over the island," I said. "We should talk to her, but I'm pretty sure she has an alibi for the time of the murder. Unless the poison was slow-acting?"

I'd been working under the assumption he was poisoned and died immediately.

"No more than ten minutes between the dose and death," Lilibeth said. "It would have to be strong or spell-enhanced."

"Phillip gave us a list," Mark said. "He keeps pressing for updates. Should I be telling him what we're doing?"

The question was directed at Mrs. V, but D and Lance shook their heads. Lilibeth didn't react, but I could read her reluctance in the pool of indigo that swirled through her emotions.

"Not yet," Mrs. V said. "I am concerned he will do something rash. When we are sure we have the killer, we will invite him to the interrogation."

"The list?" D asked. "I put it in the spreadsheet. Are we interviewing them before we head out to the animal thing?"

Mrs. V pulled out her phone and brought up the image of the paper. "This might not be all of our returning or visiting witches, but a good place to start."

"Do you know any of them?" I asked.

"Why wouldn't I know everyone on the island, Cossi?" she said with a withering look at me. "The Blueseas visit often enough that we're all acquainted with them. They run a potions and tea shop in Edmonton. She's related to Alder Bark some generations back."

"Both would have the knowledge to distill the poison," Lilibeth said. "And they might have known Martin."

"Most of us would be able to create a solution strong enough to kill," Mark said. "We'll interview them today."

"Deidre Little and Herman Busch were out exchanging techniques with other witches," D said. "I remember her saying some California community wanted to improve their weaving skills. And Herman was my music teacher. Didn't he go to London to some fancy arts place to learn some old-time songs?"

"Whatever else they did will come out in the interviews," Mrs. V said. "Everyone on this list might have run across Martin Light in their travels."

"What about the other two?" I asked.

"Izzie was ready to find a mate," Lilibeth said. "She told me last festival that it was time to bring new blood in and that she was going to seek out someone. Did she come back with a boyfriend?"

"It doesn't say," D said. "Do you want to talk to her?"

Lilibeth agreed to take that interview. "I get to be the first one to hear her adventures."

"Tony Reed," Lance said. "I'm glad he's back. Dolph was

looking for new metal fencing for his garden. I'll let him know as soon as we clear Tony from our suspect list."

Lawson mentioned him when we chatted. I didn't know if that meant anything more than Tony was well known and liked.

So, our new action list was to do more interviews and then update each other. This investigation was far more broken-up than the previous ones. In the past, mostly it was Mark doing his thing and us doing ours, together.

"Okay we need to assign the interviews," Mark said.

"Not to me," Mrs. V said. "People seem to find me intimidating. I like it that way."

"I'll talk to Tony," Mark said. "Cossi, you should come with me. I think he was your father's friend."

It made me happy to have someone who would talk about my parents, also scared he would tell me things I didn't want to know.

"D? Who do you want?" Mark asked. "Deidre, Herman, or the Blueseas."

Too many people to get to before we joined Destroyer and our furry path-makers.

"I'll take Herman this afternoon," D said. "I still need to contact my dad."

"I'll take the Blueseas," Lance said, "and I'll talk to Deidre if I have time. If not, first thing in the morning."

"What about Ms. Flor?" I asked.

"Do you know where she is?" Mark asked.

"I can find her. If we need to meet Destroyer at dusk, you and I can talk to both leads. I mean, they aren't suspects yet, right?"

"Not yet," Mark said, "but let's all be careful. The more people we interview, the more likely one of us will be talking to a murderer."

Part of me wanted the killer to be someone who'd been away from Henbane. The people I'd met here seemed like family. Too many of them had already died. And if Martin was killed by someone who lived off-island, it meant my suspicion was wrong. The murders were not connected.

"I'll fit in Deidre," Lilibeth said. "I would drop in on her anyway to hear about her trip. This way, I can do it without Mom, and we will get all the interviews done today."

I had no idea who or where Lilibeth's parents were. Or any of my friends, come to think of it. I'd been so busy between murders and getting The Inner Spell open that meeting family went well below the bottom of my to-do list. I would try to be a better friend when we solved this latest murder.

28

I sent a text to Ms. Flor and arranged to meet her at her chalet for a chat. I had no idea where Destroyer would send us for this magical path, but nothing was too far from my business.

Ms. Flor had been here when Martin was killed, and she'd benefited from his death. If being on the committee was a benefit. She just didn't strike me as a killer. More a party girl than anything. And she was my first guest.

If she turned out to be the killer, that was another tie between me and the murders. They started when I'd arrived, and the little we'd learned suggested the reason for the killings would be found that evening twenty years ago, when my mother made her mistake.

I guess the biggest reason I didn't want it to be her is that I liked her. She'd been fun and had more depth to her character than I'd noticed in party girls when I went to university. I could imagine her seriously pondering a spell, or doing research, or any number of things that didn't include drinking and meeting up with strangers.

"Tony is at home," Mark said, ending the call he was

making as we headed back to the bike park. "He says he'll see us there."

"What did you tell him?" I asked.

"The truth," Mark said. "No point in doing anything else. If he's innocent, lying might make him angry enough not to tell us something. If he's the killer, we need him worried or running."

Since he was the one to remind us that any of the people on this new list could be the murderer, I didn't think it was prudent to give Tony notice.

"That he's a suspect?" I moved Beulah from her parking space and rolled her to the road.

Mark moved beside me on his official bike. Black, with a trailer hitch. "That we want to ask him about Martin Light."

I didn't have any other questions as we rode towards the small cottage on the east-facing edge of the island.

THE COTTAGE WAS TUCKED in beside a huge barn-like structure. The windows and doors of both buildings were thrown open. I put Beulah beside Mark's bike in the rack. I guess being a metalworker meant you didn't just have a wooden hitch for the bikes. This was a black iron sculpture with vines and spokes that looked like tree branches to rest the bike against.

"Come on out back," a voice called. "House and work-shop are still pretty musty. Spells can only do so much."

I followed Mark around to see a slight man with an overdeveloped upper body lounging on a cast iron chair. A mug of beer sat on the matching café-style table. He poured two more mugs for us without asking if we wanted some. "Grab a seat. I'm watching that little family of hedgehogs just now. Missed that about Henbane when I was gone. The wildlife."

Mark introduced me and we sat. I looked at the hedgehogs and thought at them. "Are you working with Destroyer?" If this was part of the path leading to the murder site, it would be nice to know.

"Not yet," one of them answered. I couldn't tell which one. "We are watching this witch because he is new."

I let them know it was his home, and they thanked me. I guess when a witch was gone for a while, the shorter-lived animals didn't know them.

"Lance says his Alpha will call you for some work," Mark said. "Is the forge set up yet?"

Small talk to get Tony off guard?

"I'm sure you've been told this more than a few times," Tony said to me, "you look just like your mother."

"Thank you," I said. "Yes, some people have mentioned it. Did you know her?"

He laughed. "Your dad and I were rivals for her attention for all of three days. She chose him and I had nothing to say about it."

I smiled because I didn't know what else to do. His words carried a lot of emotion. From him a general joviality that had a gray stain to it, maybe a little regret over not winning Mom.

From me?

My emotions were always a little hard for me to get beyond the surface. Maybe because I felt them, not just saw them as colors or vibes. I was curious about my parents, but we weren't here for that, and glad that he wasn't my dad for some unknown reason — maybe just because I'd lived with the one I had. And the same sadness as every time I thought about them. Both dead because we lived outside the paranormal world.

"Did you know Martin Light?" Mark asked. "Or maybe saw him on the island?"

"Poor guy, first time on Henbane and he's dead before he can enjoy the freedom of living only with us witches and shifters around. We were on the same boat crossing from the mainland. Didn't talk much. Heard he was doing some kind of research with a bunch of witches here."

"There is a committee," Mark said. "No one seems to have known him other than a few calls before he came."

"Phillip did," I said.

Had Mark forgotten that, or had I messed up some kind of questioning strategy? I didn't get a side-eyed look, so whatever I'd done it wasn't too bad.

"Phillip Raziel. There's someone I haven't thought of for a while. Still brewing tea and trouble?"

"Owns the bookstore," Mark said. "Has for a while."

"Yes, he did when I left, but he always had a little sideline going. Teas, in particular. He had a subtle hand. We played a few pranks when we were kids. Giving the brattiest a dose of forgetting, or a day-long hiccupping session."

"I guess that's why he's so particular when I make tea," I said. "I live over the store in his spare room. He was my mentor when I arrived."

"I haven't seen evidence that he's been pranking people," Mark said. "Maybe being on the council made him stop. I seem to remember a lot of the older witches had sidelines. Did you?"

Tony waggled his hand. "More of a conflicting path than anything. I like the way metal always does what I want. And it needs physical strength as well as magic. For a while, Mrs. V thought I was going the earth witch path all the way."

"So, you can grow plants where they don't usually thrive?" I hadn't thought of doing more than one thing. The Inner Spell took all my time — all of it not being used to solve crimes.

"No, but I can enhance their innate purpose. Like I can grow a potato that gives comfort. Not just the usual carbohydrate contentment, but real ease for a troubled heart."

"Effie will be knocking soon," Mark said. "She'll want to stock your produce as soon as you can get a crop ready."

"She always wanted me to farm rather than just mess around with what I thought might be fun. Too late or too early now to get anything planted. Maybe I'll put in something for a wintering. I need to get working on the forge. Is there anything more?"

We left with about as much progress as we started. Nothing he'd said made him a suspect. Reminiscing about my family could wait until we'd caught the murderer.

29

I had an hour before we were set to meet Destroyer and his little army of rodents. That left fifteen minutes before Ms. Flor was expecting me. Plenty of time to grab a sack of feed for the food boxes around the island and fill some of them. I'd get to the rest after we found the place Martin was killed.

"We can update while we do the search," Mark said as we pedaled back to the village. "Any hints as to where we start?"

I thought at Destroyer and he said, "The garden where he was found. We will be ready for you. The prey animals say to start there because you might learn something. I told them it would be better to tell us where the path ends, but they are not yet my obedient servants."

"And they will not be," I said. "You can't control all the animals."

"We will see." He cut off communications.

"He's out of control," Mark said with a laugh when I passed on the information. "But the animals have a point. We might miss some evidence if we don't follow the path."

"Are there animals Destroyer won't be able to command?" I had a sudden picture of him herding his obedient subjects to the mouths of their hungry predators.

"Don't believe him when he says these creatures obey him," Mark said. "And I'm not sure he can control the horses, goats, or sheep. They seem to have a bit of difficulty following instructions from their witches."

I'd totally forgotten that there were other animals I could talk to here. "Where are they? I mean, there's a lot of Henbane I haven't seen. And I know there must be cows for the milk, and other regular farm animals."

"I'll take you around when we have time," he said. "I need to go check with Roy and think over what Tony said. He wasn't lying exactly, but he did avoid a few hard questions."

"His emotions were a little shaded," I said, remembering the gray that dulled his joviality. "Is he a suspect? Like a real one, not just the 'everyone is a suspect' thing."

"That's what I need to look into. I have some contacts who can confirm his story. And I guess all the stories we get once we know what the others found out in their interviews."

"I'll let you know what my guest has to say."

We parked our bikes, and I headed off to grab a pair of the seed and nut bags I kept in Lilibeth's store. With two, I could balance them on Beulah's frame so I didn't need to hitch up a trailer.

The food boxes were set just off the main path across the island. I started at the far end from my place and filled the ones at the entrance to the shifter village and the solitary area. The two at The Inner Spell were fast, and I'd do the other two on the way back tonight. Maybe if people stopped committing murder, I wouldn't have to set up an economy based on food for information.

Ms. FLOR WAS SITTING on one of the stump seats. Elias had crafted the original roughly chopped trunks into chairs. Heavy, but they could be moved if needed. The central fire pit was cold. She had a pint of beer in one hand and her phone in the other.

"Would you like a pint?" she asked as I walked over. "That Lance Volk would be very popular on the mainland. Microbrewing is all the rage. Part of me wants to help him distribute there, and the other part wants to keep it local so I can get some when I visit next. Oh, I should probably talk to you about reserving rooms for a longer stay. You know, I'm representing the witches in the wider world. I was honored when the protector asked me. Did you suggest it?"

She took a breath and I leaped in with answers. "I'm fine, thanks. I have something later that requires me to have a clear head. Yes, I knew you were asked to join and I did suggest it. And I'm happy to sit with you and reserve a chalet or a room. And I'm really glad you are having fun on Henbane."

"It does feel a little disrespectful to enjoy myself when poor Martin is dead in such a dreadful way." She downed half her beer in one gulp. "But then, I am still alive, so it might be best to enjoy it."

"Did you know him well?" I didn't want to get into a philosophical discussion about grief.

"How well do we know anyone?" she asked. "I knew of him in our circles. I am a historian, and he was a researcher. Our work put us together occasionally. If I had known he was coming here, I would have offered to travel with him. He was private and quiet, but when you got past his shell, Martin was intelligent and had a wry sense of humor."

"Did he have any enemies?"

Zinnia's the first person to admit she knew our victim more than just by name. Even Phillip, who called him a friend, hadn't been able to tell us much.

"Rivals, I'm sure. We are an insular group, academicians. Nothing murderous, but petty feuds can turn, I suppose."

I'd encountered a few problems in university with professors who fought over things like publication credits. I don't know why I thought paranormal academics would be different. Nothing I'd encountered since I arrived supported that assumption.

"Do you know why he would stay with Phillip rather than one of the members of the community?"

"Phillip invited him to stay," Zinnia said. "If he'd asked me, I would have suggested this place. But you sold out fast, so I suppose it wouldn't have worked."

That's not what Phillip said. I'm sure he told me Martin asked to stay with us. Maybe I misheard, a lot had happened since he informed me we'd have a guest.

"I sold out because of your review," I said. "Thank you for that. A new business is hard to get off the ground."

"Oh, my dear, you have no idea how interested people are about the famous Henbane community where the protector lives."

"What kind of history do you study?" Maybe her background would help me work out if she was a candidate for the suspect or cleared list.

"It's a wide field, but I concentrate on lost skills. We in the wider world are more worried about staying hidden than preserving heritage sometimes. So, I scour folklore and old books, some from Phillip's store, for hints of disciplines we've let slide."

"That must bring you into contact with a lot of people," I said. "It sounds fascinating."

"Sometimes. But often I spend months following a thread only to find nothing at the end. Now, do you have any more urgent questions? Because I have a date."

"Nothing urgent, and I have to go, too. We'll look at the calendar another day. Have fun on your date."

30

W e stood in Azalea's garden watching a line of squirrels form at the gate. It was a bit like a horror movie where rodents swarm a victim to squeaks and ominous music. The squeaks and chittering were there, but not the soundtrack. None of it turned into words for me. I hoped it was just the sheer volume, or a secret internal language I hadn't learned yet, rather than my powers going away.

Destroyer landed on my shoulder without warning. "Are you waiting for an invitation? Get going. They'll lose interest soon."

I passed it on, adding a warning not to step on anyone, and we headed out. Keeping alert for anything we'd missed when searching before.

"It's likely we won't see any evidence until a bit farther along," D said. "We would have noticed something so close to the body."

"The creatures found some items that they are convinced will solve the case," Destroyer said. "I leave it to you to decide."

The light dimmed as we passed the houses along the path. Solitary witches didn't all live in remote caves. In fact, I was pretty sure none of them were actual hermits, or anyone on the island was, for that matter. Most of the solitary houses were comfortable and equipped with all the modern conveniences, like television and Wi-Fi.

"This is a leaf that doesn't belong," a young mouse said. He or she, I wasn't going to look to find out, held a green spear bigger than he was towards us.

"I think it's a tulip," I said. "Do any of the witches near here grow them?" Way out of season for tulips, but on Henbane, earth witches manipulated growing seasons. Only in small ways. They couldn't control the weather. Even D, who's power was weather, couldn't do much about it.

Mark reached down and took the leaf when I explained what the mouse said.

"Not a tulip," he said. Then he took an evidence bag out of his backpack. "Thank the mouse. It could be Lily of the Valley, but why would someone drop a leaf here?"

I told the mouse he'd done a good thing and reminded him to get his payment. He giggled and suggested that forgetting about food was impossible.

We walked along while we all offered reasons for the killer to discard the foliage.

"Maybe Martin didn't die on the first dose," Lance said. "Had to be re-poisoned, then stabbed in Azalea's garden?"

"Not likely," Lilibeth said. "Most of the cases I had time to research suggested it would take a large dose to kill, but it could be fast. Managing a dose would be too tricky. The best way to do it is distill the poison and hold the victim until he died."

"Coincidence," D said. "Lots of people grow it as a border plant."

We were making progress, but the light was fading. Mark handed out flashlights to help with the search and make sure we didn't trip on some hidden root or rock.

"Keep the lights out of our eyes," Destroyer said. He launched himself off my shoulder, almost dumping me on my butt with the force. "I will see you at the end."

"Do you think he's doing this for theater?" Mark asked. "He could tell us where this goes. We could mark the path and search again later."

"Possibly," I said, "but we're here now."

By the time we reached the end of the path at a large rhododendron bush somewhere toward the cliffs on the west of the island, we'd accumulated three buttons, a glove and a shiny piece of foil.

"I'm surprised people here litter," I said. "Nothing looks like it will help."

"Not litter," Mark said. "I'll keep them as evidence, but I'm pretty sure these are things taken by birds. Little trophies."

I didn't press him or ask Destroyer about it. I stared at the bush in front of us. The typical growth pattern that left spaces like domed rooms inside. I knelt and pushed aside a branch. Nothing to indicate Martin was ever there.

"What are you doing?" Destroyer landed beside me on the ground.

"Looking for clues," I said. "This is the end of the path."

"No," he said. The tone in my head was like eye rolling at our stupidity. "Around the back."

We squeezed past the bush to see a shack in a small clearing.

"Why did the chipmunks stop at the bush?" Our path had changed from squirrels to mice, to raccoons, to chipmunks along the way. Even walking slowly, it took us less than a half hour to get here. I suppose the killer would want to minimize the distance they needed to move Martin.

"How would they get the body past this?" Lilibeth asked. "We had to squeeze."

"Wait for me," Mark said.

He didn't go toward the shack like I thought. He circled the bush and checked the ground. "The branches are damaged," he said when he finished. "The killer came back and cleaned up any fibers or shreds of clothing. But someone forced their way through. Maybe enough to get scratched up."

So, this was the place, unless more than one witch had a reason to use this hut.

"And the animals?" I asked Destroyer.

"Spell. Only affects land creatures. They stop here. I fly over."

How would the killer know about the animals investigating? Especially if they were from off Henbane?

Time to figure that one out after we search the shack.

"Is there a spell on the building?" I asked after I relayed Destroyer's answer.

Mark took out a single lens, like a monocle without the hanging strap. He scanned the area three times.

"Nothing to change the look," he said as he put the lens away. "Traces of old magic, nothing active except the discourage spell at the bush."

"What is that?" D asked, pointing to where Mark had put the lens.

"I bought it on the mainland," he said. "Shows magic as a cloud of sparks. I tested it, and it's reliable."

"What if a normal human got their hands on it?" I pushed away the sudden fear that we were too late to protect the mainland communities.

"It needs magic to operate," Mark said. "Not a danger."

He led the way into the shack. It was as dilapidated inside as the outside promised. There was a small table in ruins on the back wall. One cup must have been shattered against the left wall by the mess on the floor. Another lay in two pieces next to the table.

Lilibeth knelt to sniff at the pottery shards. "Lance, come check this," she said, standing over the shattered pieces.

He bent over the largest shard and then pulled back. "Poison and ginger tea."

"So, now we know where and how," I said, "but why would Martin agree to come here?"

31

There was no way to answer that question, and unless Mark could cast a spell to reveal the name of the witch who made the tea, we were stuck. The pottery shards were all too small to give us fingerprints. And I didn't know if magic could dissolve the oils needed to make a print or change the print so it pointed to someone other than the killer.

"What now?" I asked. "We have the site, but I don't see anything leading to the killer."

"I'll search the area with some of the shifters," Mark said. "It's better not to have too many people involved."

His emotions were locked down again, and I hated the idea of leaving. But did my decision to trust him mean I couldn't argue?

"What about using the animals?" I asked. "Could they help?"

"It would mean you have to stay," Lance said. "Destroyer can't stick around; he's got to sleep. And he's the only one you can talk to long distance."

"He's right," Destroyer said.

"What about Roy?" I asked. "Since the 'ground animals' can't get past the bush, will he be able to help you?"

He couldn't talk to Mark like he did to me, but Roy had been absent for a while.

"He's on another assignment," Mark said. "Watching the dock for anyone trying to leave."

"How will he tell you?" Roy understood enough to take orders from Mark, but watching for someone trying to escape — which was exactly what Mark meant by leaving — wouldn't help if he had to find me to pass on the news.

"That's why I need you at home," Mark said. "Lance will be able to search, but the three of you don't have any talent in that area. If Roy sees anyone leaving other than the people who would normally need to go back and forth for festival preparations, then he'll find you, or tell some other animal to pass it on. You text me. I deal with it."

That seemed overly complicated.

"But whoever it is will already be gone," Lilibeth said.

Mark smiled in a way that told me he'd out-thought us.

"Not for the witch I have on the mainland waiting. I've given this new 'animals as informants' thing a lot of thought. Even if the killings stop, and we all hope that's going to happen, having access to a widespread and intelligent force will make my job so much easier."

I guess he had way more experience at using magic than I did — everyone I met these days did. "Could I carry some animals through the bush? Give them a chance to inspect the interior before I go?"

"I'll come with you," Lilibeth said. "I can tell if it's safe."

Between her power of knowing what animals need and mine to talk to them, we'd be able to get someone through.

"I will sleep here," Destroyer said. "If there is need, I can be woken." He hopped through the gaping door, and I watched him fly up to a branch on the hazelnut tree in the yard.

Lilibeth and I went through the rhododendron. Two squirrels and a chipmunk volunteered to try pushing through the spell. We tucked them into our pockets for safety and made our way back.

"Sick, but not too bad," one of my squirrels said. "Gone now. We search."

I told Lilibeth and we placed them on the ground.

"That's something to note," Lilibeth said. "The spell made them feel ill. Without a strong reason, no animal would go near the place. None of them would notice they were being kept out. More proof that someone knows your talents?"

"Is it a signature? Or just the poison still here?" I crossed my fingers that we'd found a clue, no matter how weak.

"The poison wouldn't affect them," Lilibeth said. "It isn't something that can harm you by breathing it in. They would know to avoid eating anything that harmed them. Especially since no one is starving. You're doing a good job of feeding them."

"So, could the sick feeling tell us who made the poison? Or the spell to keep them out? It's not a sure thing that the same person did both."

"I'll have to think it over," she said. "Look."

Our searchers were scrambling to be the first to get to us.

"One speaks," I said, hoping to avoid an onrush of squeaky voices. "All get paid."

The bigger squirrel sat up and looked me in the eyes. "Smell of metal. Burned metal."

I didn't remember seeing anything that would generate that smell. There was something that would smell like metal, though. "Blood?"

"Not dead eater," the squirrel said. "Metal is metal. It pokes us or tries to get in our way."

I thanked them and offered to carry them back through the barrier.

"Not needed. We can go through this way. Only to keep us out, not in."

The three animals scampered away.

I told Lilibeth what I'd learned.

"Lance should be able to find it," she said. "It's probably faint, but now we know it's there, he'll be able to locate the source."

We went back in and waited while Lance slowly circled the room.

"The animals were all over, so we don't know where they found the scent." Mark pulled an evidence bag out, ready to collect whatever Lance found.

"Here," Lance said. "Iron. Very faint. I wouldn't have found it without a pointer. Not blood. In fact, he wasn't stabbed here. I would be able to tell."

"Does that help?" I asked. "Is it rare?"

"Iron is all over the place," D said. "It could be an old ritual knife or a frying pan. But it's something we didn't know before."

"What about the burned part? Is there a ritual that burns metal before it's used? Like passing it through a flame?" I could easily imagine a frying pan getting burned, or at least the contents.

"It's too faint," Lance said. "Yes, there are some purification rites, but there's a difference between using fire to sterilize and burning the metal."

"Tony would know," I said. "We should ask him if it's possible to burn metal without a forge."

"He's moved up the list from person of interest to

suspect," Mark said. "So, we need more if we're going to interrogate him. Let's get this done and we can talk at break-fast. At The Howling Place? Sheena does a great pancake."

We agreed and let Lance and Mark continue the search. Three more shifters passed us on the path as we rode toward home.

32

"Long day," Philip said when I entered the apartment. "Any closer to finding the killer?"

"Maybe," I said, "but Mark wants to keep the investigation quiet for now."

"I understand," he said. "I don't like being left out, but I would probably be advising him to keep the residents ignorant of the facts."

Did he have to make it sound so manipulative? I guess I should be happy he'd gone from trying to take over the investigation to accepting that Mark was capable.

"I have some tea ready," Phillip said. "Your parents liked this so much, I used to bring it along with the other one."

I knew he visited my parents, but not that he brought presents. And what the heck was 'the other one'?

"Have I had their favorite yet?"

He'd made me a lot of different ones, but mostly just an herbal tea with a licorice taste. I kept my coffee consumption to what Jan made because I wasn't about to get an espresso machine when I was being supported by the council.

"You enjoyed it when I made it there," he said. "I haven't wanted to raise your memories of your childhood. So, no."

"I have good memories," I said. "I'd love some."

He put a cup in my place at the table and took a jar of honey from the windowsill. "I know you don't usually use sugar, but this one is so much better with a little sweetness."

He poured, and I was suddenly transported back to the kitchen in our old house. Lemon and mint with just a hint of black tea in the aroma. This wasn't a memory of when we had the visitor — Phillip. This was the three of us, on the couch. A day when the windows were gray with rain. The fireplace blazed, and we listened to dad reading us a book.

"What was the other tea?" I asked.

His emotions went from warmth and comfort to nothing.

"You don't have any memories of my visits?"

I wanted him to tell me the truth, but I didn't know how to convince him to just go ahead and say it.

"Just voices in the kitchen. Did you give me the other tea when you came?"

He actually struggled to keep from telling me. I watched him swallow and then look around as if he would find another topic of conversation.

"Phillip, it's in the past. Just tell me."

The frustration of knowing there was yet another secret in my past had me wishing he would stop waffling.

"Yes. I came to assess the effectiveness of the tea and adjust as you grew."

His eyes widened. He hadn't expected to tell me.

"What did it do?" I had an awful feeling I knew the answer, but I willed him to tell me.

"Suppressed your powers," he said. "For your protection.

Now it affects only your third power. Your mother made me swear to keep it from gaining strength."

They knew what my third power was and took it away? I could barely look at him when I asked, "Do you know what it is?"

"No. They wouldn't tell me. I've been using the tea to keep it from rising. It's harder now that you're using the other two powers."

"I want you to stop doing it," I said.

"Whatever that power is, your mother was afraid of you using it," Phillip said.

"When I lived as a non-witch," I said.

Like Carly, the killer in our last case. Her mother suppressed her shifter nature.

"If you are sure," he said.

"I am. What does this tea taste like? The suppressing one?"

"It's the licorice blend."

"And when will I know it's not working?"

"Your power will rise. I advise you to tell your new mentor, so she is prepared."

33

I went to my room after Phillip's confession. I couldn't trust myself to say anything more, and I didn't want to live with the repercussions of having a full out fight about his actions. I slept badly because every time I came to the edge of unconsciousness, I jerked away, wondering if I could feel my new power.

I didn't hang around for the usual cup of tea or piece of toast. I wasn't sure I'd trust anything Phillip offered me until my power was uncovered. Destroyer told me they hadn't found anything overnight, but that a shifter was sent to watch Tony's home.

Mark would fill us in when he arrived at The Howling Place. Beulah was waiting for me to take her out for the ride.

I knew she was just a bike, but at that moment, I'd take a relationship with anything I could trust. Because the revelation from Phillip made all my suspicions about Mark come back to life. I'd forgiven him when he'd asked for help, but there was nothing to say he was doing much to end the extortion. Avoiding the contacts from his mysterious blackmailer when he knew he should let D trace them just made things harder.

By the time I parked Beulah at the shifter pub, I'd managed to talk myself off the ledge. Mark was more open now about the caller. Having this murder to solve was probably getting in the way of freeing him. And I didn't want to distrust him, so I wouldn't unless he gave me a reason.

Mark was waiting outside the bar when I walked up. He held out his phone and I could see he was on a call. To the blackmailer, if I remembered the number correctly.

He gestured for me to go inside and put the phone to his ear.

"I can't talk to you about that," he said.

Then he noticed me still standing behind him and glared while making a shooing motion.

I pulled the door open, and he turned away to keep talking. I wasn't going inside to miss his half of the conversation.

"Sure, I can tell you before we make it public."

"No, I will not jeopardize the case."

"Let's face it, if you wanted to use that against me, you would have."

"You try to hurt anyone, and I'll come clean to the council."

"Yes."

Then he looked at the screen. The call was over.

He turned to see me. I tried to put an innocent expression on my face, but it didn't feel right to me. It probably looked stupid.

"D was tracing it," he said. "Let's go in and I can tell everyone at once."

I was the last to arrive. I couldn't tell anyone my news, mostly because it had nothing to do with the murder or the blackmail, as far as I could tell. And because one thing

Phillip got right — I had to tell Mrs. V first. She wasn't at the table.

D was staring at his laptop screen. Lilibeth talking to Lance. No one seemed worried or excited. We must have still been stalled.

"Any luck?" Mark asked as he took the chair next to D.

"This is someone who knows how to disguise his location. Or her, I guess. The voice sounded altered. Was it always like that?"

"Yes, I keep thinking it's a man, but that might not be the case." Mark pulled out his notebook and placed it on the table. "Did we order?"

"Pancakes and bacon all around," Lance said. "Coffee and water. Privacy on the side."

There were a few tables occupied in the bar, and all were shifters. And all of them could hear us talking.

"How? The privacy, I mean."

"A spell," Lilibeth said. "Muffles our voices past the next table. Sheena won't let anyone take a seat close to us."

"So, what's the update?" Lance asked. "I checked with Dolph. Sexton is being observed, nothing suspicious. He was making jewelry all day. New hobby, apparently."

"One that uses metal," Mark said. "And Tony?"

"He's been cleaning out his home all day," Lance said. "The forge was lit at lunchtime, but I guess it takes a while to get up to metal softening levels. If his fires have been out for years, he couldn't be the source of the burned iron stench."

"How do we know he didn't light it earlier?" Lilibeth asked.

"We don't," I said, "but maybe a few of my friends would be able to answer that question."

I thought out to Destroyer.

"Rabbits," he said. "Not very reliable, but I will ask. Too late now to send someone. The new fire will cover any old one."

I passed it on and listened while Mark shared our interview with the others. "What did you learn?" he said when he finished.

"Deidre isn't our killer," Lilibeth said. "I checked her story and it's true. She was on her way when the murder happened. And I don't think Izzie is capable of the kind of thinking this killer needs. She was not successful in finding a mate, and hoped the festival would give her another chance."

Two people off our list.

"I talked to Herman," D said. "He was reluctant to get into details. I'm not sure he's a suspect. But now that we know about the metal thing, I did see him repairing an old organ. Not sure it's made of iron, but maybe."

"The Blueseas were here," Mark said. "They're staying with the Barks, and they're not our murderer. No lies. They're sweet and a little frail."

"Ms. Flor isn't our killer either," I said. "She's been vetted by Mrs. V."

"That leaves your dad," Mark said. "Not a suspect, but did he know anything?"

"No answer at their number," D said. "I'll try again later."

Mark looked up from his notes. "Is that normal?"

"They get busy. I left a message, and they usually call back within a day."

"How long has it been?" I asked.

If his parents were out of communication range, did it mean anything for our case?

"Yesterday, after we split up," D said.

"Is that the first time you contacted them?" Mark asked. "Recently."

Had D's dad turned from person of interest to suspect? In the murder case or in our search for whoever was trying to control Mark?

D checked his phone log. "Two days ago. And they haven't called me back. I guess we've been so tied up in this investigation I didn't realize."

34

"Try again," Mark said. "If that doesn't work, I'll call on the office phone. I'm not sure I want to use it for much right now. If you cloned my mobile, maybe my mystery caller has, too."

Probably had.

I searched my memory of the calls and texts that Mark sent over the last few days. There were too many about the case between all of us, and Mrs. V. Evidence and clues.

"If it is cloned, what would they have learned?" I asked as D placed the call.

"I thought about it when D cloned it. I've tried to be careful not to put details in texts or talk about the case on my phone. If whoever they are did manage to link phones, I don't think they'll get anything beyond calls and texts."

I could look it up later, when we weren't chasing a killer.

D was talking, so he must have made contact.

"You need to come home," he said. "There's been another murder and... Martin Light, did you know him? No, you aren't a suspect... I try not to listen to gossip... why don't you come back?"

A long speech came over the phone. D grunted occasionally to acknowledge the information.

"Keep me posted," he said and then ended the call.

"Where are they?" Lilibeth asked. "Too far to get back?"

"Vancouver," D said. "They were on their way home. Wanted to surprise me. Dad got sick and he's in the hospital. Mom says she'd never heard of our victim."

"How bad?" Lilibeth asked. "Does he need a witch to come?"

"Mom can take care of any magic," D said. "He got a bad case of food poisoning, then an infection. She says it will take time for him to heal. They'll let me know when they're on their way home."

"I'll check the farms and house more often," Lance said. "Probably some tidying up needed. And if Batiste needs to recover, he shouldn't come back to a musty house."

"So, we can cross them off the list?" I asked. "They have a good alibi."

"Yes. It would be different if they knew Martin Light. In that case, I'd go over to talk to your mother," Mark said. "I guess we keep looking into the strangers and returnees. And the committee members, and everyone else on the island at the time."

"The committee members?" Lance asked. "It's hard to imagine they'd have a motive."

"Maybe they didn't want Martin as the representative," D said.

"Or, they don't want to solve the problem," I added.

"Or someone is controlling one of the members," Mark said. "We think the same person is behind all the murders, right?"

"I guess my mind doesn't go to the dark side so easily,"

Lance said. "If we look at the evidence from all the cases, do we have any idea who might be behind it?"

I'd been running that exact question in my head since the second murder without coming close to an answer. I'd thought it was because I didn't know how to be a witch. Not just the magic, but the whole culture. My first few days of thinking all witches and shifters were kind and helpful — with the exception of Mrs. V — and generally good proved completely wrong. Witches and shifters were people with all the contradictions and weaknesses of every other human on the planet.

"Mark, what if the person trying to control you is the same person behind the killings?" D asked. "We don't know for sure how many separate plots we're coming up against."

My information about Phillip suddenly became important to the investigation. I couldn't tell anyone else before I let Mrs. V know.

"I need to make a call," I said. This wasn't something to send in a text.

I went out to the porch and dialed her number.

"I'm busy," she said in greeting.

"This is important," I said. I told her about Phillip suppressing my powers.

"Interesting," she said. "Do you believe him? That he'll stop?"

"You know him better than me," I said. "Should I? I can avoid eating or drinking while I'm there. I can stay in my room, because of the protection bag."

"The Phillip I knew was trustworthy, but people change."

So, she didn't know any more than I did. "I'll be cautious. And when the festival is over, I think I should move out."

"Prudent. Why was this so urgent? You are coming tonight for your lessons, yes?"

"Unless we catch the killer. I need to tell the others about it and thought you should know first."

"Correct." She ended the call.

I stood for a moment staring at the screen and trying to figure out if she was annoyed with me or Phillip, or both, or the whole world.

Deciding it could be any or all of them, and either way I couldn't do anything about it, I went back inside. The waiter was refilling coffee and water when I sat. When he left us alone, I told the others everything about Phillip.

The silence afterwards was colored with a blue wave of shock and disbelief. Today, I didn't want to see what people felt, but I couldn't turn it off. The blue shifted to an orange spiky anger from Lilibeth and D. Mark and Lance radiated a sour purple shade that tasted like betrayal.

Great, now I could taste emotions? I needed a way to manage it, or I'd never enjoy food or drink again.

"He is my council representative," Mark said. "Even so, it's against our rules to suppress a power without permission."

"My parents gave him permission when I was a child," I said. "He just didn't ask again when I came. What's the punishment?"

"I'll have to look it up," Mark said. "Although Mrs. V probably knows."

"He said it was to protect me when we lived as normal humans. I can understand that."

I couldn't forgive him for continuing to feed me the tea, but I didn't want him banished or whatever.

"I was going to handle it myself, but when we started talking about the possibility the person behind the murders and the person controlling you being the same, I thought of him. He kept his actions secret, and you could look at it as controlling me."

"He's on the council," D said. "They swear oaths. It can't be him."

"Yeah, but those oaths are supposed to keep him from doing things like suppressing powers without permission," Lance said. "You can't keep this a secret, Cossi. Even if Mrs. V says you should. Dolph needs to know."

"I wonder," Lilibeth said. "Keeping it secret might just be the right thing. The council will want to know why your other powers came out as soon as you arrived. That's what's supposed to happen. The only one suppressed is your third power. What if it's one that needs to be stripped?"

I didn't like the sound of that, and everyone had their emotions under control again, so I had no way to tell what they really felt.

Mark looked around to make sure the spell was still keeping our conversation private. "His oaths would stop him from overtly doing harm to any paranormal community. He could have convinced himself that continuing until someone told him to stop was the right thing. I don't agree with what he's done, but those oaths can't be broken."

"Come!" Destroyer screamed in my head.

35

"Where?" I could sense his direction, but not the exact location.

Lance's phone pinged with a text before Destroyer answered. "Dolph says Seela isn't responding. She was watching Tony."

"Not metal witch house. He is leaving," Destroyer said.

"Where do you need me?"

"On way to boats. Near your home, not boats in shifter or earth places."

"We need to get to Roy," I said. If he knew Tony was coming, he might get hurt trying to stop him alone.

"I'm going to see if Seela is alive," Lance said. "I guess one of our questions just answered itself."

We split up, Lilibeth joining Lance in case this Seela needed medical help.

I raced behind Mark and D, wishing the path was wider so we could talk.

"He is ahead of you," Destroyer said. "Go faster."

I passed it on and then saved my breath for pedaling.

Destroyer kept up a running commentary. "Dog is alert."

We turned onto the path to the main village, and I saw someone speeding their bike to the parking lot.

"Witch is hurt."

We dropped our bikes in the empty lot at the end of the street. Tony was limping toward the boats, waiting to go to the mainland.

Mark shouted for Tony to stop.

A flash of mottled fur came from the side and landed on Tony's back.

Roy stood on him when he hit the ground.

"Dog is brave," Destroyer said. He swooped over my head and landed next to Tony, giving him a nasty peck on the ankle. "Bad witch."

36

A small crowd of witches and shifters joined us. Three stepped out and held Tony so Mark could handcuff him. Then he was hauled up and dragged to the cell in Mark's home. No one actually harmed him. Well, the hit from Roy and the peck from Destroyer, but they weren't life-threatening.

Mark contacted Doc Rene, who said she was dealing with Seela and would come when she was finished. Tony had knocked the shifter out, and he was a murderer, so I guess he wasn't high on her list.

Dolph joined us in the hall outside the cell. He let his emotions flow, or it might have been his alpha energy. There was none of the rage I expected. He was mad at Tony for hurting a shifter, but not enough to rip the bars open and attack.

"The other council members are on their way," Dolph said. "D, you will act for your father."

D stepped forward to join Mark and Dolph near the cell.

"You are lucky a shifter heals quickly," Dolph said to

Tony. "Your spell would have been sufficient, so why did you need to break her jaw?"

Tony held up his arm. I was wrong; he had been hurt, but not by either animal I'd seen. A bite left him with bruises that looked like teeth marks.

"She was stronger than I remember shifters being."

We waited in silence after that. Mrs. V joined them first, then the other council members until we couldn't see past them to the prisoner.

Lance slipped out and then returned with three chairs. He placed them against the wall and then helped Lilibeth to stand on the seat. I didn't wait for a hand, so in moments we were looking over the heads of the council, waiting for what I could only think of as a show to start.

"You might as well tell us everything," Mrs. V said. "Why did you kill him?"

"I was told to. I barely knew the man." He licked his lips and swallowed. I kept a close eye on him to make sure we weren't about to watch another witch die from some kind of spell.

"Who told you?" Dolph asked.

It looked like the rest of the council were happy to leave the interrogation to the alpha and the protector.

Tony licked his lips again. "I don't know."

The door opened and Doc Rene slipped in. She elbowed people aside until she reached the cell. "He is injured. Let me in and I'll tend to him."

"He is a murderer," Mark said. "We need to restrain him first."

Mrs. V tossed a powder through the bars and then Mark cuffed Tony's uninjured arm to one of them.

"He won't be able to use magic for an hour," Mrs. V said

to the room. Possibly for my benefit. "He was bitten by the shifter you attended and possibly bruised from Roy, who stopped him from leaving."

"And a peck on his ankle," I added. "Destroyer didn't like him."

My familiar had flown home to roost for the night as soon as Tony was restrained.

"Are you going to watch?" Doc Rene asked.

"Yes." Dolph didn't offer any reason.

It took her less than half an hour to apply a salve to his bruises, sterilize and bandage both bite and peck. "You don't deserve any pain relief," she said. "Seela was just doing her job."

Then she left, I guess to other patients, or she didn't want to hear his excuses.

"How could someone force you to kill and remain anonymous?" Mrs. V asked.

"I'm fuzzy," Tony said. "I came back looking forward to renewing old friendships. I remember talking to Mark and Cossi. I remember arriving and reaching home. Between those events. I have only scraps."

Dolph turned to us. "Are you certain this is the murderer?"

"I did it," Tony said in answer. "Not saying I didn't. One of the scraps is me pushing a heavy cart, but I didn't make a poison. I had blood on my hands when I got back. But until this morning, I have no other memories. I woke from a nightmare. I knew without a trace of doubt I was the killer. I had a fresh shard of memory of holding a knife. Covered in blood."

"We need to discuss," Mrs. V said. "Keep him safe. We will use your office, Mark."

Whatever they talked about was a secret. D was in with the council, but we weren't linked like Destroyer and I were.

"I'm hungry," Mark said.

"I'll make tea," Lance said, "and a snack if you have anything in the cupboard."

Roy barked from the kitchen.

I translated to human. "He says there's cheese in the fridge and crackers in the cupboard next to it. He will be happy with some cheese."

"Not too much," Mark said. "It doesn't sit well in his stomach."

"What do you think they're talking about?" I asked. "He confessed."

Tony tugged at his cuffed arm. "Probably how long to wait before I head off to prison."

"We'll find out soon enough," Mark said. "There are a lot of spells and potions that could blank out his memory, some not even requiring magic."

"You think a normal human found their way here?" Lilibeth asked.

"Not a chance," Lance said as he walked back with four plates and cups on a tray. He pushed the paper plate under the door to the cell and followed it with a paper cup of water. "Nothing you can hurt yourself with."

He handed us our own China plates and cups.

"I didn't mean that," Mark said. "I mean, anyone could have ordered a drug or grown the components. Remember what happened to Jeffery? Maybe the person behind it was perfecting the dose. Just taking out enough memory, not all of it."

Before we could get into more of the subject, the council returned. Mrs. V walked alone to the cell while the others stayed a little back. There wasn't much room to separate in the hallway, so we could hear everything she said.

"You will be transported to prison today. When you arrive, one of the witch guards will try to help you remember more."

They walked out, leaving Mark to make arrangements and D to tell us what happened in the meeting.

"I'm sorry," Tony said. "I wish I knew why I killed him."

37

When the council left, except for D of course, we gathered in Mark's kitchen to talk.

"So, what can you tell us about the council's decision?" I asked.

"I can't tell you everything," D said, "but I can say they are suspicious that someone is pulling strings. The two things we voted on were how to properly deal with Tony's sentence, since it was clear there was a lot missing from his story, and we unanimously voted not to press for names. That's the point where the last two died."

"He'll be picked up in a couple of hours," Mark said. "Shifters will escort him to their dock for the transfer. It's not busy, so less chance of him getting away."

"I feel sorry for him," Lilibeth said. "I don't know if I believe he killed anyone. Do you really think there's a chance he took the blame for someone else? Not just under a compulsion?"

"Give me a minute," I said. "I remember one of the cop shows I used to watch had a plot about something like that."

"It's fiction," Mark said. "You know you can't believe what you learn from television shows."

I ignored him and kept searching. Of course, I wasn't looking for the plot. I was looking for the drug. Then I'd go to a reputable site for the real details. Unfortunately, there were so many episodes of the show that it would take me hours to find the one I wanted. But the searching helped me remember.

Zombie drug. The search took me to Scopolamine and Devil's Breath, which were different names for the same thing.

"There is," I said, "a chance he was drugged into taking the blame, I mean. This powder is used by criminals to get people to relinquish their money or other things. A dose would make Tony do what he was told."

"Unfortunately, that includes killing Martin Light," Mark said. "Is there a way to detect it?"

I searched again to find out if there was a test. "Not now, it's been too long."

"How is it made?" Lance asked.

"Seeds from a plant," I said. "So, it could be done here."

I showed them the image of the Angel's Trumpet."

"Several plantings all around the island," Lilibeth said. "Another clue that doesn't help."

"We are ahead of where we were a couple of days ago," Mark said. "We know that someone is behind all of it. We know there's a question about Tony's guilt. We can't ask him about names because we need him alive. But if he was drugged, he's not the killer, even if he did end Martin's life. He's the weapon."

"It's late," D said. "I'm going to visit my dad in the hospital tomorrow. There's one thing we need to try before I go to bed."

As far as I knew, there were no loose ends. "Did you learn something?"

"We found a spell," Lilibeth said. "I'm not sure it will work. We need to try to release Mark from the control of this mystery person."

"We looked when I realized we weren't going to be able to trace the calls," D said. "If we can't catch the blackmailer, we should be able to protect Mark."

"We think there's probably more than protecting his secret going on," Lilibeth added. "Like a spell or a hex that keeps Mark vulnerable."

"I'm ready to try anything," Mark said. "Let's do it."

"Be careful," Roy said to me. "Magic is not a blanket to be lifted, more like a web that tangles."

I didn't think the warning was just for me.

"Roy is worried about complications," I said.

"I don't care," Mark said.

"The spell is to sever outside magic," Lilibeth said. "It should only act on what you don't know is there. Your connection to Roy is part of you. Your magic is safe. We won't know if the spell worked, but you should feel something. The next time whoever this person is contacts you, it won't work the way they expect."

I guess it was better than nothing, but we still wouldn't know who the person was, and I wanted a name. The more I thought about it, the more I believed the blackmailer and the person behind the killings was the same individual.

"How long have you been under their control?" I asked.

"About ten years," Mark said. "Nothing bad until the murders started."

I couldn't leave him vulnerable just to feed a hunch. "Do we need anything?"

Lilibeth pulled out a selection of powders, sticks, and

potions from her backpack. "Stand in the center of the room," she said to Mark. "The rest of you make space."

I tried to memorize every step of the spell as she performed it. This one was far more complex than any I'd cast so far.

Lilibeth grabbed some bowls from Mark's cupboards. She mixed ingredients and put the contents in four pots from her supplies. Then she laid them around Mark. "North, south, east, west." She murmured the words as she placed them.

Pulling out a lighter, she walked counterclockwise around, lighting each bowl and then touching a bundle of herbs to the flames. By the time she was finished, Mark was standing in a cloud of aromatic smoke.

"Let the pots burn down," she said. "Then it's over."

We waited, but it didn't take long. The smoke wafted toward Mark and seemed to disappear into his clothes. Okay, 'seemed' is probably not right. It did soak into him.

D picked up the pots and went to the sink. He placed them in and then turned on the kettle.

"How are you feeling?" he asked.

"No different," Mark said. "I guess we wait until I get a text or call."

I looked at Roy. "Do you see anything different?"

"Smells like plants, but it is still him."

I let the others know.

The kettle boiled and D poured the water over the pots, muttering a cleansing spell.

"I have to go to my lessons," I said. "Mrs. V doesn't believe in letting events get in the way. I have to drop by my room and grab some books."

"See you tomorrow," Lilibeth said. "Don't the rest of your guests arrive in the afternoon?"

At least I had the morning to get their rooms ready. Oh, and work on some details for my festival booth.

38

I was surprised to find the bookstore closed. Phillip usually kept it open quite late, and it was only just dinner time.

I walked past the store to the side entrance and ran to the top to grab my books. Mrs. V didn't set a timetable, but her expectations always seemed to be five minutes before I arrived, so I was always late.

Philip was in the kitchen, head over a bowl of steaming water, a towel creating a tent to contain the benefits. I could smell the usual cold clearing suspects, menthol, eucalyptus, and honey. He hadn't shown symptoms when we were at Mark's place only an hour or so ago.

"What happened?" I asked. "Do you need the doctor?"

He spoke from beneath the towel. "I think it's a reaction to finding my friend's murderer. No need to bother Doc Rene. I'll be fine soon enough."

The room was warm from the treatment, but he had a long-sleeved shirt on and long pants, his hands tucked inside the towel tent. I didn't think a stress induced cold would come on so quickly, but maybe it was a witch thing. He was certainly old enough to make his own decisions.

"I'm heading to Mrs. Vestum's," I said. "Let me know if you need anything."

I couldn't leave him without a little help, so I sliced lemons and took the honey jar and plate to the table. He'd already put the oils for the aromatics to hand.

"You can just reach for supplies," I said, "but you should probably go to bed soon. Sleep is the best way to recover."

He thanked me and slipped his hand out to touch the jar. The back of it was bruised, badly, the colors standing vividly out against his normally pale skin. Then he pulled his hand back under the cover, as if he hadn't meant to move.

"Did you fall?" I could only think of two reasons for those bruises, and Phillip didn't strike me as the kind of man who punched walls to relieve his anger.

"Banged it," he said. "Your mentor is waiting."

I grabbed the books I'd read for my next lessons and left. I'd be home again to check on him before too long.

The walk to Mrs. V's was only a few minutes if you actually jogged trying to meet an unspoken deadline. I was almost at her door when my phone pinged with a text.

Mark, to all of us. *It worked. Got a text. Ignored it. No headache. Thanks.*

MRS. V HANDED me a cheese sandwich when I arrived in her kitchen. For the first time, no comment on how late I was, overt or implied.

"This has been a long day," she said. "I think we will put aside the general studies and try two spells I've been researching."

"You got the text from Mark?" I asked, excited to learn more spell work.

"He told me what you did for him," she said. "We will see what the repercussions are of his freedom."

I ate the sandwich, not wanting to go down that path. Today, I wanted to just be happy for Mark.

"Did you make note of Lilibeth's work?" she asked. "You are keeping a spell journal? If not, start one."

"I've been making notes of everything, so I guess the answer is yes. What are we doing tonight?"

"First, the talismans," she said as she placed the bag on the table. "I have been giving them a great deal of thought. There is an old spell of discovery that might work. Are you ready?"

I nodded and cleared the dishes from the table. She'd lectured me enough about making sure my casting area was clear of contaminants.

"Will it show the real symbols?"

"If the ones we see are actually there," she said. "You have assumed that the current appearance gives us a hint to the original."

"We have to start with some ideas," I said, "but I will clear my mind of expectations."

While I centered my thoughts on openness, Mrs. V placed the talismans in a circle at the center of the table. She pulled out a parchment — yes, a real parchment, not paper made to look like it.

"You will read this," she said. "I am here to instruct and support. The spell must come from you because these objects have become your possessions."

Like they could choose. I didn't comment. Who knows? Maybe they could.

The parchment had three words.

Revelare, Veritas, Nunc.

"I feel like I'm in a Harry Potter book."

"Well, this is real Latin," she said. "The age of the language gives it power."

She told me the pronunciation, which was pretty much what I thought.

"The spell requires you to invest power from your own store of magic."

"Which one?" I asked. I only had two I could use, and I wasn't sure either related to this spell.

"You have magic to use. You've done it before. When you use a spell. Think of it as intention. As you perform the spell, think deeply about what each component is intended to do."

She placed three packages of powder in front of me. A blue, a green, and a yellow. They all looked like kid's finger paints. She gave me the instructions and a glass of water.

"I don't want you coughing or anything," she said. "Drink the water. Then, cast the spell."

Okay, so I wasn't about to dab my fingers into paint.

I drank the glass of water in one go.

I closed my eyes and thought about the words. My job was to say the word and dust the talismans with the matching powder.

I took a breath and let it out.

I reached for the blue package and thought about the concept of revelation. I put the powder in my palm and blew out the word *revelare*. The powder floated over the talismans and settled. There was no residue in my hand.

I took the green and repeated the procedure with the word *veritas* and finally with the yellow and *nunc*.

"Look," Mrs. V ordered.

I opened my eyes to see the stones flickering. It was so

fast I could barely make out the differences. The symbols changed, but all of the options had a picture of something. The color of each changed through the spectrum. Then everything settled back into our usual bag of stones.

"Draw one," she said. "It may still have worked."

I took my notebook and a pencil from the counter and sketched a random choice. I turned the drawing toward her.

"Progress," she said with a smile. "I see what you see, and the drawing matches the object."

"But we still don't know who they belong to."

How was this progress?

"One level of deception is lifted. We will be able to research more clearly now."

"Did I make a mistake?"

"No. This is a complex magic. You did well. I will continue to find spells to uncover more of the truth."

"Okay, at least I cast the spell right," I said. "What was the second thing?"

She swiped the talismans into the pouch. "You clean while I secure these again. Then we will look for your third power."

39

She walked away before I could ask any of the thousand questions that popped into my head. Mostly variants of 'why now'.

I wiped up the leftover powders and then cleaned the tabletop with hot rosemary water. Mrs. V was taking longer than I expected to come back into the room, and I started imagining all the ways she could have changed her mind.

When I put away the cleaning supplies and placed the cloths in a pot for boiling she appeared in the doorway.

"Take the pot outside," she said. "I need all traces of other spells removed."

I took the pot with the water to the patio and placed it at the edge of the stones.

"You are doing something," Destroyer said in my mind.

He should have been sleeping at this hour.

"A spell to reveal my third power," I said.

"The old witch knows what she's doing," he said. "I am close and will try to watch."

"No. You need your sleep," I said.

"There is someone I need to bring," he said. "We will be there when the spell is over."

I went back into the room. Mrs. V had a pot of tea steeping on the table and three saucers of herbs. I told her my familiar was on the way.

"We will be done quickly," she said. "Perhaps it will be good to have him with you either way."

I sat at the table facing the patio. I'd see when Destroyer arrived, and whoever he brought.

"What if my power is a bad one?"

"I have taken precautions," she said. "Now, Phillip told you the spell to suppress is a tea. The pot contains just Ceylon Black. It is neutral. I think one of these, or possibly two, are the ingredients he used."

"Why can't you just ask him?" This seemed overly complicated.

"Two reasons. I am unsure of how much we can trust him, and we may want to keep the results of our spell secret."

Sneaky.

"Okay, so what do we do?"

"Smell the herbs and tell me if you recognize anything."

"The licorice, definitely. I remember the taste, and Phillip admitted it. The leaves, I don't think so. What are they?"

"St. John's Wort. It was a guess."

"The seeds, but only a few. Is that Nigella seed?"

"Yes. Now close your eyes and think about the tastes. What else is in this tea?"

I did as I was told. I went back to a memory of being in my home in Vancouver. My father in the kitchen talking to someone — I now knew it was Phillip.

"Tea and licorice and... bitter pepper... honey... something that didn't belong. Too savory. I took another deep breath and followed the thought. "Thyme, but with a little lemon. Not lemon in the tea, but in the herb."

"Bitter pepper was the seeds. Lemon thyme. Interesting." Mrs. V stood and sorted through the jars in her spice cupboard.

"I will make what I think is his tea. Do not drink it. The two days since you made him stop should be enough to weaken his spell. We don't want to give it a boost."

Her first attempt was close. I gave her instructions, and we had the right combination in a few minutes.

"Do you make an antidote? How long before it works?"

"It will work, or not, immediately," she said. "I will be back in a moment."

I walked over to the patio door and peeked outside. It was too dark now for me to see Destroyer arrive. I slid it open to check the backyard.

"I will tell you," he said. "Finish working."

"Shut the door," Mrs. V said.

I did so and returned to my chair.

She passed me a vial of liquid the color of bile. I looked closer and saw bright pink specks swirling around.

"Don't think about it," she said. "Drink it all down. I suggest you try to avoid tasting it."

That did not sound great.

You want this, I reminded myself. I pulled the cork and tossed the contents back like a shot of Tequila, feeling very glad the vial was small.

The world faded in and out a few times.

"Did it work?"

"Yes. I need you to empty your mind and try not to panic."

"You know that increases the chance of panic, right?"

"A witch learns to control their fears."

I really wanted her to tell me what my power would do, but she was my mentor, and I needed to trust her.

I centered my thoughts on a cool lake.

"Good. Now hold onto that calm. Your third power will need to be suppressed again."

I knew it!

The lake in my mind shimmered and rippled as if a meteorite had smashed into the center. I struggled to hold onto my calm.

"What is it? I mean, I agree to be suppressed, but I would like to know before you do it."

"You can force someone to obey you."

The image in my mind shattered.

"It is a simple thing to teach you to manage it, Cossi. The reason it is dangerous is that you will be tempted."

My memory wandered back over times when people changed their mind around me for no reason. Or rather, a reason I didn't recognize. They changed their mind because I really wanted them to.

"Okay, are you going to make the tea?"

"Cossi, open your eyes, please." The words were said kindly, which was disconcerting.

I opened them and saw her crushing the vial into shards. "What are you doing?"

"I'll burn these later," she said. "Your power will come in handy for our next task. I will suppress it when we find out who is threatening our lives with these killings."

"And then? Will everyone know my power?"

"The spell to suppress it requires more than one council member. But if you wish to keep it quiet, we will honor that request."

"We are here," Destroyer announced, giving me no choice but to drop all the questions that flooded my mind.

I opened the patio door, and he strutted in, glancing around for food or water or beer. Behind him, a kitten wobbled over the threshold.

"Who is this?" Mrs. V asked, bending down to cradle the kitten. "Oh. A lynx kitten. And she spoke to me."

"Her familiar," Destroyer said. "Name is Tulip. Her mother sent her. Now I need a drink before bed."

Henbane Island's annual festival is in full swing, and Cossi Fortuna is ready to enjoy the festivities—until a whispered warning shatters the illusion of safety.

Use the QR code below to grab your copy of A Spell to Discover now!

FREE BOOK

Claim your copy of Magic Will Out when you sign up for my newsletter and follow Cossi as she seeks answers to her past. Use the QR code to claim your copy now.

ALSO BY THIS AUTHOR

For more books by Poppy Bridgeman

scan the QR code below.

ABOUT POPPY BRIDGEMAN

Hi, I'm Poppy Bridgeman a pen name for P A Wilson Why did I pick a pen name Well the new witchy cozy mysteries are very different from my other books, which tend to the gritty. So, Poppy came along to write these gentler stories.

If you're interested in P A Wilson, read on.

Perry Wilson is a Canadian author based in Vancouver, BC who has big ideas and an itch to tell stories. Having spent some time on university, a career, and life in general, she returned to writing in 2008 and hasn't looked back since (well, maybe a little, but only while parallel parking).

She is a member of the Vancouver Writers Social Group, The Royal City Literary Arts Society, and The Surrey Writing Workshop. Perry has self-published several novels. She writes the Madeline Journeys, a fantasy series about a high-powered lawyer who finds herself trapped in a magical world, the Quinn Larson Quests, which follows the adventures of a wizard named Quinn who must contend with volatile fae in the heart of Vancouver, and the Charity Deacon Investigations, a mystery thriller series about a private eye who tends to fall into serious trouble with her cases, and The Riverton Romances, a series based in a small town in Oregon, one of her favorite states. Her stand-alone novels are Breaking the Bonds, Closing the Circle, and The Dragon at The Edge of The Map.

For more information
www.pawilson.ca
pawilson@pawilson.ca

ACKNOWLEDGMENTS

People think that the process of writing is solitary. That's not the case for me. I have help from so many people it would be hard to acknowledge everyone, but I'll give it a try.

The support and inspiration I get from my writer's groups is incalculable. The Vancouver Writers Social Group opens my mind to other ways of telling a story. The Royal City Literary Arts Society gives me the opportunity to meet and share with other writers who have more knowledge than I do. The Other 11 Months group is where I learn about getting the words on the page. And my critique group who helps me find the best parts of the story I want to tell. Thanks to all of the members of these great groups.

Last of all, but definitely a huge part of the process, my beta readers. These are the people who love stories and are willing, and more than able, to tell me if my finished story is ready for you, my readers.